Amanda glanced ... cation form on the floor.

'What's *this*?' she asked, grabbing it before I had a chance to stop her.

'Nothing,' I yelled. 'Gimme it back!'

She fended me off with one arm.

'Hah!' she crowed. 'I *thought* so! No wonder you've raced to get to the mail first every day! You were waiting for *this*!'

'What if I was?' I said, desperately trying to retrieve the entry form before Amanda had the chance to start reading my responses.

'You've been making fun of me and my friends for the past *two weeks* about this,' Amanda yelled. 'And all the time you were getting a form of your own. Of all the two-faced people, Stacy! And I caught you!'

Little Sister books published by Red Fox

Star Search

Allan Frewin Jones

Series created by
Ben M. Baglio

RED FOX

For Bethany and Crystal

A Red Fox Book

Published by Random House Children's Books
20 Vauxhall Bridge Road, London SW1V 2SA

A division of Random House UK Ltd
London Melbourne Sydney Auckland
Johannesburg and agencies throughout the world

1 3 5 7 9 10 8 6 4 2

First published in Great Britain by Red Fox 1996

Set in 12/14 Plantin

Printed and bound in Great Britain by
Cox & Wyman Ltd, Reading, Berkshire

Papers used by Random House UK Ltd are natural, recyclable
products made from wood grown in sustainable forests. The
manufacturing processes conform to the environmental regulations
of the country of origin.

RANDOM HOUSE UK Limited Reg. No. 954009

ISBN 0 09 968881 6

Chapter One

'I must, I must, I must increase my bust! Elbows out, palms together and pu-u-u-ush! Pu-u-u-ush! PU-U-U-USH!'

That was my thirteen-year-old sister Amanda.

'Ow! My *ear*!'

That was me. I'm eleven. No, I didn't get whacked in the ear by Amanda's enormously expanding *bust*. I got hit by a Frisbee thrown by my friend Fern.

'You're supposed to keep your eye on the game, Stacy,' Fern, the Frisbee thrower, laughed without even a hint of sympathy. 'Not your *ear*!'

We were enjoying a lazy afternoon in our back garden. By *we*, I mean me and my friends, Pippa, Fern and Andy.

Up near the house, Amanda and her friends, Rachel, Cheryl and Natalie, were sunbathing and trying to look like a bunch of super-cool Californian beach-babes.

I'd looked around when I'd heard Amanda's voice. She was sitting up cross-legged on her towel, with her arms in front of her, elbows out and palms together. Doing *bust increasing* exercises, would you believe?

That was when Fern's Frisbee had whacked me in the ear.

'Stacy loses one point,' Andy said as he picked up the Frisbee. 'One more drop and you're out of the game, Stacy.'

'That doesn't count,' I complained. 'I wasn't ready.'

'It's in the rules, Stacy,' Pippa said.

I took the Frisbee from Andy. We'd see who was going to be out of the game! I twisted myself around like a corkscrew then hauled off with the hardest throw I could manage, straight at Fern.

She ducked and my intercontinental Frisbee-missile went zooming up the garden.

'Yeowww!' Cheryl howled as the Frisbee ricocheted off her behind. She glared round at me. 'You did that on purpose!'

'No, I didn't,' I called, trying not to laugh. 'But it's kind of hard to miss a target that big!'

'Why, you little—!'

'Guys! Fresh lemonade! Come'n get it!' It was Mom, calling to us through the open kitchen window.

It was a really hot day and my mom's home-made lemonade is the *best*. Which is why we nearly trampled one another into the ground as we ran for the back door.

'Bring a glass out for me, Stacy,' Amanda ordered as I ran past her.

'Oh, sure, your majesty,' I said. 'Anything you say.'

'Thanks, Mrs Allen,' everyone said as we each picked up a glass of lemonade. My mom sure does know how to make guests feel welcome.

We went and sat on the patio. Amanda gave me an expressive glare.

'I guess we'll just have to get our own,' she said, getting up. 'Some people are so selfish it's just not true.'

She went into the kitchen with Rachel, Cheryl and Natalie trailing along after her. Rachel, the carrot-headed gibbon-girl, Cheryl the sniggering hyena, and prissy Natalie with her ultra-long ash-blonde hair and her gopher face. Known collectively to people of discern-ment as the Bimbo Brigade.

Fern picked up an open magazine from Cheryl's beach towel. It had pictures of super-fit tanned women wearing leotards and getting into strange positions.

' "The summer is here," ' Fern read. ' "It's

time to trim those hips and thighs, tighten those buns and take your beautiful body down to the beach." '

'I don't want to take my beautiful body down to the beach,' Andy said.

'What beautiful body?' Fern said. 'Your body is about as beautiful as a length of hose!'

'At least I'm not *stunted*,' Andy said.

'I am not stunted!' Fern said. 'Haven't you heard: small is beautiful.' Well, I wouldn't exactly call Fern beautiful, but she is the smallest of us. She makes up for it in other ways, like being the *loudest* of us, for instance. She's got out-of-control short blonde hair that always makes her look like she's just jumped out of bed. And she wears some pretty way-out clothes, too. (Her mom and dad are kind of hippies and I guess some of it rubbed off on Fern.)

Andy *looks* like a regular person, but he's got this *thing* in his brain that makes him a little crazy at times. Not *bad* crazy, more kind of out-of-his-tree crazy.

Pippa is the big brain of our gang, and she looks the part, too. She's tall and gangly with long black hair tied back in a thick plait. Her mom is a college professor.

Me? I'm the smart one. A girl has to be smart to survive living with my sister,

Amanda. I know I said Pippa was the *brain*, but there's a big difference between being able to spell *February* and use words like *bombastic* and being a really smart person. Besides, there are a whole bunch of ways in which Pippa is totally dumb. You'll probably find some of *those* out as we go along.

Fern sat up and got into the bust improvement position.

'OK,' she said. 'Here goes. I must, I must, I must increase my bust.' She waggled her elbows in the air and pushed her hands hard together. 'Guys?' she said. 'Are they getting any bigger yet?'

'Oh, wow!' Andy said. 'They're enormous. Help! I'm being crushed by Fern's gigantic chest!'

'It says that regular exercise will . . . uh, *enhance* your bust development by up to fifteen per cent,' Fern read.

'Fifteen per cent of nothing is still nothing!' Cheryl said. 'And I want my magazine back, if you don't mind.'

Amanda sat down and peered at me over her sunglasses.

'Don't you kids want to go play down the other end of the garden?' she asked. 'Go play in your cute little sandbox.'

'Not when we can stay right here and annoy you,' I said.

'Oh, wow!' Rachel suddenly shrieked. 'Oh, wow, guys, listen to this!'

She had the local newspaper spread out on the ground in front of her. I guess she must have been looking to see if there was a cartoon page.

' "Search for a star!" ' she read. ' "Intelligent, photo ... uh, photo-*gen*-ic, uh, chair-uh-ismic, cheer-as-motic, uh, matic." ' She stopped, frowning. 'What a totally stoopid word!'

Pippa leaned over her shoulder. 'The word is *charismatic*,' Pippa said. 'It means having a great personality.'

'I knew that,' Rachel said, swatting Pippa away with one flapping hand.

'So how come you couldn't *say* it?' Pippa said.

'The print is too small,' Rachel said.

'The print is the same size as all the other words,' Pippa pointed out.

'Do you want to die young?' Rachel snarled.

'Oh, for heaven's sake,' Cheryl said. 'Give me that!' She whipped the newspaper out from under Rachel's nose. 'Now, let's see. "Search for a star! Intelligent, photogenic, charismatic, industrious young all-American

10

person wanted," ' she read in a dramatic voice. ' "Do you have all the above qualities? Do you want to be the face of Blowbubble Bubble Gum? Do you want to be a star? If the answer to all these questions is yes, then contact Thelonius P Appleby and make your date with fame!" '

There were a few seconds of complete silence while we all took this in.

I leaned over to take a look at the ad. It took up a quarter of a page, outlined with coloured stars and with huge, bold print. At the top was the familiar Blowbubble logo: a pink elephant blowing a huge red bubble with its trunk. At the bottom of the ad was a telephone number. I recognized the area code. It was the same as for my dad's head office in Chicago.

'What does it mean?' Natalie asked.

'It means they're looking for a young person to be a star,' Rachel said. 'A star! A *young* star.' She pointed to herself. '*We're* young,' she said. 'One of us could be a star!'

'Yeah, but starring in what?' Amanda asked.

'Bubblegum ads, I guess,' Cheryl said. 'You know, on TV, maybe.'

'On billboards!' squeaked Natalie. 'Imagine it: *my* face, coast to coast on every highway!'

11

'Yeah,' Fern said. 'The face that crashed a million cars!'

'Way to bankrupt a company!' Andy said. 'They'd never sell another pack of gum!'

'Hold up,' Amanda said, 'let's get *real*, shall we? If this Appleby guy is only advertising in the local paper, this *isn't* going to be some huge great international deal, is it?'

'Blowbubble Bubble Gum sells all over the country,' Pippa said. 'Thelonius P Appleby is the boss. I read it somewhere.'

'Maybe he's advertising in local papers all over America,' Cheryl said.

'We may as well forget it, then,' Natalie said. 'There are going to be thousands of people going for it. *Hundreds* of thousands.'

'Great attitude, Natalie,' Amanda said. 'Don't you remember? Ashley Mercury started off his whole career in a TV commercial for a new brand of running shoes. And now *he's* a multi-millionaire movie star!' She spread her arms out. 'One of us could be the next Ashley Mercury!'

'Ashley Mercury is a boy,' Rachel said. 'We're girls.'

'I'm not,' Andy said.

'Who's talking to you, bug-face?' Cheryl snapped.

'I don't see where the ad says *girls only*,' Andy said.

'Nobody, but *nobody*,' Cheryl said, 'is going to want to see some ugly geek face staring out at them from the TV.'

'I guess that takes you out of the running, then,' Fern said.

'Why, you!'

While they were all arguing I fixed the telephone number in my head and quietly got up and went inside.

'What's all the noise out there?' Mom asked as I headed for the hall. 'You know I don't like it when you start arguing with Amanda's friends.'

'We're not arguing,' I said. 'We're *discussing*.'

'Get bent, nerd!' I heard Cheryl yell.

'That's what I like to hear,' Mom said. 'A reasoned exchange of opinion.'

I went into the hall and took the phone down off the wall. I sat on the stairs and tapped out the number that had appeared at the foot of the ad. While those guys out there were arguing about it, I was going to find out exactly what Thelonius P Appleby wanted.

Chapter Two

A super-cheerful woman's voice answered at the Chicago end of the phone.

'Thank you for calling the head office of Blowbubble Bubble Gum,' she said.

'Oh, hi,' I said. 'I was just—'

'If you are responding to our advertisement, please press *one* at the end of the message. If you are calling for any other reason, please hold the line. Thank you for calling.'

It was a pre-recorded message. I don't know about you, but I always feel like a total idiot when I find out I've been trying to talk to a *machine*. I pressed one.

The same woman started speaking again, but this time I didn't say *hi*.

'Thank you for responding to our advertisement. Blowbubble Bubble Gum is launching this year's advertising campaign in the home town of Thelonius P Appleby. To show his deep and abiding love and regard for the town where he grew up, the face of Blowbubble

Bubble Gum this year will be a young person from Four Corners, Indiana. If you would like more information about this prestigious and high-profile advertising campaign, please leave your name and address at the end of this message. Please remember that entrants must be under fifteen.' Then there was a *beep*.

I guess that was when I was supposed to leave my details. Not that I had any intention of entering their dumb contest. I'd seen things like that on TV shows. All the kids are like, total spoilt monsters, and the one who always wins is the one with the biggest smile.

And there's one thing I'd noticed: none of them had a teeth brace like me. And none of them had flat, boring, mousey-brown hair and freckles.

I hung up the phone and went back into the garden. The argument was still raging out there.

'They won't want dorky *kids* like you,' Cheryl was saying to Fern. 'Unless it's for a diaper ad!'

'A diaper ad!' Rachel snorted. 'Hurr, hurr!'

'The ad says *intelligent*,' Fern yelled. 'So that blows all four of you out of the water from day *one*!'

'And I suppose *you're* the brain of America!' Natalie squeaked.

15

'They'll be looking for someone with a real good personality,' Amanda said. 'Good looks, a great personality and a smile that never stops!' She smiled so widely that her ears shook hands around the back of her head.

'Is that your idea of *personality*?' Andy asked. 'You look like you need to use the bathroom.'

'Go suck a drainpipe!' Amanda said.

'Where do you think they'll hold the try-outs?' Cheryl said. 'Not *here*, surely? Hey, maybe contestants will be flown to Hollywood, or somewhere.'

'Why Hollywood?' Pippa asked.

'Why not?' Cheryl said. 'That's what happened to Ashley Mercury. He went in for a shoe commercial in Hollywood, and the next thing he knew he was a film star.'

'I don't think anyone will be going to Hollywood,' I said. 'The company's head office is in Chicago.'

'Huh!' Cheryl said. 'Listen to know-it-all Stacy. So how come you're suddenly such a big expert on where Blowbubble Bubble Gum's head office is?'

I stooped and picked up the newspaper. I folded it up and put it under my arm, taking my time.

'I thought everyone knew *that*,' I said. 'A person would have to spend their life with their head in a bucket not to know the head office is in Chicago.' I gave Cheryl a big grin. 'Or don't you agree, bucket-head?'

'She just went and asked Mrs Allen!' Natalie squeaked.

'No, I didn't,' I said, giving them my very best superior looking-down-my-nose stare. 'And I happen to know that Thelonius P Appleby was born in Four Corners.'

'He was?' Pippa said. 'I didn't know that.'

'He sure was,' I said. I was enjoying this. It's not often that I know something that even Pippa doesn't know. I guess the *power* of knowing a little about Thelonius P Appleby went to my head. Which was why I decided to invent his life-story on the spot.

'He . . . uh, was born in Roseway,' I said, 'and he started off as a paper boy. And after three years he'd saved enough money to buy a one-way ticket to Chicago.' (Hey, not bad!) 'He arrived penniless and spent the first few months at the train station carrying people's bags and living off the tips.' (I could almost *see* the poor ragged guy as I made it all up.) 'And two years later he was the head of the biggest bubble gum company in the whole of Chicago.'

There was a brief, impressed silence.

'How?' Andy asked.

'Huh?'

'How did he go from carrying people's bags at the train station to running a big company in *two* years?' Andy asked.

'Uh, by the use of . . . uh, intelligence, charismatic-ness, industrious-ness and er, stuff like that,' I said.

'Boloney!' Amanda said. 'You're just making it up. The guy would only have been about seventeen years old!'

'That's right,' I said. 'He won the Youngest Person to Run a Big Company Award. It was on the news and everything.'

'You are just such a total fibber!' Amanda said.

'Oh, yeah?' I said. 'So I guess that I'm making it all up about Thelonius P Appleby wanting a person from Four Corners for his advertising campaign. And I guess I'm making it all up about the fact that I just *called* the number on the ad and got all the details.'

'Wait a second,' Cheryl said. 'Are you telling us that this Thelonius P Whatsisname guy is *only* looking for young people in Four Corners? Like, nowhere else at all?'

'That's right,' I said. 'He wants to show his love and respect and some other stuff I can't remember for the town where he was brought up.'

The four Bimbos looked at one another.

'Gimme that paper!' Amanda screamed at me.

'Get off!' Rachel yelled. 'I saw it first.'

Cheryl came diving at me and I had to take a flying leap sideways to avoid her. 'I want that number!' she hollered.

'What's it worth?' I called as I ran down the garden, waving the folded-up paper at them.

Hello, folks, and welcome to the big race of the day. As I take up the story, it's Superstacy in the lead, with Hyenaface close behind, followed by Gibbongirl, Airhead-Amanda and the Gopher in last place. And Superstacy has successfully jumped the notoriously difficult Lawnmower, and is heading for the big turn at Flowerbed. And there's been a faller at Lawnmower. Hyenaface is down, but Gibbongirl and the two other runners have managed to avoid the accident. They're gaining on Superstacy, but she's past the Flowerbed turn and heading for the Compost Pile. Airhead-Amanda has passed Gibbongirl on the turn. And now Gibbongirl has fallen. She's tripped over the hose and landed face-first in the compost. Yuckiepooo! It looks like she's out for an early shower! But Airhead-Amanda has almost caught up with Superstacy. And in a dramatic turn of events the Gopher has come around the other side of the

Compost Pile to head Superstacy off. This is a totally illegal move. But it's taken Superstacy by surprise and as she's tried to avoid being caught, she's tripped and fallen. Airhead-Amanda is on top of her. Yes, folks, Superstacy is down. It's all over. And now I return you to your commentator on the ground, Stacy Allen.

I guess trying to avoid four Bimbos all at once was a little hopeful on my part.

'Thanks for your help, pals!' I spluttered as Amanda sat on me and wrenched the newspaper out of my hand. Pippa, Andy and Fern were just standing there watching from the top end of the garden. Well, they weren't *only* watching. They were killing themselves laughing as Rachel pulled herself out of the compost pile and sat there spitting yucky compost-gunk out of her mouth.

'Gimme that newspaper,' Amanda panted, climbing off me and marching up the garden with the paper in her hand. 'Dumb kid!'

'I let you win!' I said as I sat up. 'I could have out run you easily!'

'Oh, sure,' Amanda said. She helped Cheryl up. 'Come on, guys,' she said. 'Let's go be famous!'

The four Bimbos trooped into the house.

'You OK?' Pippa asked.

'I'm fine,' I said, trying to straighten my T-shirt out from around my neck. 'You could have backed me up. We could have had those idiots racing all over the house.'

'Why bother?' Fern said. 'Let them call that Thelonius guy if they're that dumb.'

'What do you mean "dumb?" ' Pippa asked.

'Anyone who wants to act the complete dork in front of a bunch of total strangers in the teeny-weeny hope of getting themselves in some stupid commercial is totally dumb, in my opinion,' Fern explained.

'I don't see why,' Pippa said.

'You don't?' Fern said. 'It's all about how a person *looks*, right? If you look good in front of a camera, then you'll get the job. And you can be dumb as a brick. All good-looking actors are dumb: it's a *fact*.'

'Yeah, well, maybe,' Pippa said. 'But I don't see why it should be that way. Why should all the people we see in commercials be the dumb-but-cute type, huh?'

'You mean commercials should be full of ugly-but-smart people?' Andy said. 'Are you sure they'd *sell* anything?'

Pippa drew herself up to her full height, something she always did when she was preparing to come out with some big announcement.

'The way I see it,' she said, 'someone has got to make a stand for us intelligent people. We've got to show the world that it's possible for a person to be good-looking *and* smart.'

'How are you planning on doing that?' I asked. 'And who did you have in mind to do it?'

'I think that's pretty obvious,' Pippa said. 'Someone with good looks and an amazing brain.'

'But I don't want to be the Blowbubble Bubble Gum face of the year,' Andy said. 'No way!'

'Not *you*!' Pippa said. 'Me!'

We stood and looked at her.

She stared from me to Andy to Fern. And then from Fern to Andy and back to me. None of us said a word.

'What?' Pippa asked.

I looked at Fern. Fern looked at Andy. Andy looked at me.

'*What*?' Pippa asked again.

QUESTION: *How do you tell a really good friend that she's not exactly the most beautiful person in the world without hurting her feelings?*

'Pippa,' Fern said, 'face it, pal, you're about as attractive as a mule in a Halloween mask.'

Oh, right! *That's* how you do it!

Chapter Three

The next day.

> *Amanda:* 'Mom, is there any mail for me?'
> *Mom:* 'No, honey.'
> *The day after.*
> *Amanda:* 'Mom? Is there any mail for me?'
> *Mom:* 'Sorry, honey.'
> *Amanda:* 'Rats!'

Every day for a week and a half.

> *Amanda:* 'Mom? Is there—'
> *Mom:* 'No.'
> *Amanda:* 'Rats. Darn. Heck.'

Eventually.

> *Amanda:* 'Mom?'
> *Mom:* 'Yes.'
> *Amanda:* 'Rats!'
> *Mom:* 'I said *yes*, Amanda!'
> *Amanda:* 'Oh! Huh? *Wheehoo!*"

It had come at last. Finally, I wasn't going to have to listen to my sister moaning and whining about that darned letter all the time.

But I had to admit, I was kind of intrigued.

Amanda was sitting at the kitchen table hacking the long, brown envelope open with the handle of a spoon. I wandered in, making like I wasn't all that interested, just as she tipped the envelope up and a whole bunch of papers came out along with two free pieces of bubble gum.

The top sheet of paper was a letter with the Blowbubble elephant logo on it.

' "Dear friend," ' I read over Amanda's shoulder, ' "Please find enclosed the following, courtesy of Blowbubble Bubble Gum:" '

Amanda slammed her arms down over the letter.

'Excuse me,' she said. 'I don't recall inviting you to read my private and personal mail.'

'I was only looking,' I said.

'Yeah, well, *don't*,' Amanda said. 'It's nothing to do with you.'

'I'm totally sorry, I'm sure,' I said. 'I was just *interested*. I mean, if a person's sister is going to be in TV commercials and all that, then I'd have thought a person's sister would have been kind of pleased that a person was taking an interest.' I made a huffy *'hurrmph'* noise. 'But I guess a person was wrong to think that a person's sister would be pleased to know that—'

'OK! OK!' Amanda shrieked. 'You can read the darned letter. But just shut up, will you? You're giving me an earache!'

I pulled a chair around next to Amanda's and the two of us went through the Blowbubble pack.

There was the introductory letter, thanking Amanda for enquiring about the advertising campaign. Then there was a leaflet proving how Blowbubble Bubble Gum is not only good for you, but good for the environment, too. (It was something to do with natural ingredients and non-calorific sugar and no artificial flavourings and deeply boring stuff like that. After the first paragraph, Amanda let out a snort and slung the leaflet across the table.)

There was a glossy brochure explaining how the planned advertising campaign would be running coast-to-coast for the next twelve months and how the chosen 'face' would be seen by more than three hundred million people. ('Oooohhhh,' Amanda said with a shiver. 'Think of the fan mail I could get! Think of the movie deals!')

We were just reading how the person chosen would get to be seen on TV, in movie theatres, in newspaper ads, and on billboards, when the doorbell rang.

'That's James,' Amanda said. 'Hey, Mom?' she called. 'Will you get that for me? I'm really busy right now.'

'In your dreams!' Mom yelled from the living room.

James was Amanda's boyfriend. Now, to be honest, I personally need a boyfriend like I need an iron spike sticking up out of the seat of my bike. But Amanda has explained to me that at a *certain age* a girl starts noticing boys. And apparently, a girl starts to think boys are kind of cute and fun to be with.

I'm not looking forward to that at all. *But*, if I was a girl of a *certain age* and if I did start noticing boys, James Baker would be the kind of boy I'd start noticing.

He's nice-looking and smart and he's got a really good personality. Kind of *charismatic*, I guess you could say. And he's the best athlete in the entire school.

'Stacy, get the door,' Amanda said.

'Why me?'

'Because you're nearer.'

'By about two *foot*!' I said.

'Huh! *People*!' Amanda moaned as she got up. Amanda was already babbling at four hundred words a minute about the advertising stuff as she and James came into the kitchen.

'Hi, Stacy,' James said. James is the only one of Amanda's friends who says 'Hi, Stacy,' as if he's pleased to see me.

'Hi,' I said. James has got such a nice smile. If I was of a *certain age* I could really go for that smile.

Amanda showed him the letter and the brochure.

'See?' Amanda said to James. 'It's just like I told you it would be. A nationwide campaign. And the person they choose has to come from Four Corners.' She looked at James. 'It could be me!'

'Why don't *you* go for it, James?' I asked.

'Stacy, don't you have anything to do?' Amanda asked. 'James doesn't want to go for it. He wants to help *me* win.'

'Well, I don't see why,' I began.

'I'd be totally embarrassed,' James said to me. 'I'd much rather just be in the crowd cheering when Amanda wins.'

Amanda's face went all soppy. 'Do you really think I could win?' she simpered. (*Bleeecccchhh*! I hate it when she gets like that!)

'Sure, you can,' James said.

The next part explained the kind of person Thelonius P Appleby was looking for.

' "The young person chosen to represent Blowbubble Bubble Gum," ' Amanda read, ' "must personify all those fine attributes that have made American youth the envy of the world." ' Then there was a long list of *attributes*.

The *attributes* included being honest, hard-working, thoughtful, caring, and charismatic (again! They sure liked that word!), and having an outgoing, optimistic, go-getting, friendly and fun-loving nature.

Nowhere did it mention *airheaded*, which kind of put Amanda and her Bimbo friends at a disadvantage. I mean, if 'dumb as a dough-nut' had been one of the attributes they were looking for, then Rachel Goldstein would have won hands down!

But I noticed it didn't say the chosen person had to be totally gorgeous either.

' "In conclusion," ' Amanda read, ' "the lucky winner will be a young person of whom Thelonius P Appley, his home town of Four Corners, the state of Indiana, the Blowbubble Corporation, and last but not least, the entire population of America, can feel proud! Good luck to you all!" '

Amanda flipped the page over. The entry form was attached to the back.

Just then, the phone rang. I went to answer it.

It was Cheryl. I brought the phone in to Amanda.

'Yeah! Me, too!' Amanda squealed into the phone. (I could hear Cheryl squealing as well at the other end.) I guess the mail had just arrived at Cheryl's house. Did I tell you? *All* the Bimos called in for the Blowbubble pack on the same afternoon.

'I've gotta go,' Amanda told Cheryl. 'I'm going to fill the form in right this minute! Yeah! Yeah, I will. Yeah, right, good luck right back at you!' She put the phone down. 'And I hope your form gets lost in the mail.'

'Amanda!' James said. 'I thought she was your best friend.'

'She is,' Amanda said. 'But all's fair in love and war. And this is war!' She pushed the phone across the table and smoothed out the application form. 'OK,' she said, 'Let's take a look.'

It was like a regular competition form, except that there was a space at the top for a picture.

Amanda sucked her pen. ' "On the following list of personality points, please put an X next to all those which apply especially to you." Hmm. Uh-huh. Yup. Yeah, I sure am.' She went down the list, crossing every box.

'You are not *selfless*,' I said, leaning over her shoulder. 'You can't put an X in that box!'

'Oh, be quiet, Stacy,' Amanda said, almost poking my eye out as she waved the pen around. 'Go play in the traffic or something, you're getting on my nerves. Hmm. "Of the above attributes, which three do you consider most important?" I'd say ... uh ... caring, sharing and thoughtfulness.'

'I don't believe this!' I said.

The phone rang again.

I picked it up. 'Hi,' I said, guessing that it would probably be Cheryl again. 'Welcome to Amanda Allen's Fantasy World. Anything you hear is likely to be the product of a deranged mind. How can I help you?'

'Huh? What did you say?' I recognized the squeak. It was Natalie.

'It's Nat,' I said to Amanda.

'I'll call her back,' Amanda said. 'Can't talk. Filling in form.'

'Hey, Nat?'

'Don't call me Nat!'

'Amanda's busy right now.'

'But I wanna tell her I got the stuff from the bubble gum people,' Natalie squeaked.

'Give me that.' Amanda grabbed the phone out of my hand. 'Natalie? Yeah! Me, too. And Cheryl, just— huh? She called you, too? I know. I know. I'm already trying to think of a really good picture to send. Yeah, I know. I'll call you later.'

'Doesn't this kind of thing drive you crazy?' I asked James. I guess I was still trying to figure out why a nice guy like James hung out with a bubblehead like Amanda.

James shook his head. 'I think it's great the way she gets so enthusiastic about things,' he said. 'And when she gets excited her nose kind of twitches in a really cute way.'

A note from Dr Stacy Allen, psychiatrist: It was at this moment that I finally realized that the patient, James Baker, was totally and incurably insane.

Amanda slammed the phone down and started crossing the next column of boxes, which were all to do with her future plans. She put a cross next to wanting to go to college, and travel, and work for charity and enter a profession. All at the same time, knowing Amanda.

Then came a trickier part. She had to write a few sentences on why she thought she would make the perfect 'face' for Blowbubble Bubble Gum.

The phone rang *again*!

I dived on it. 'This is a recorded message,' I said, pinching my nose so I sounded like a machine. 'Amanda has already got the Blow-bubble pack and is filling it in. She will call back when she has finished.'

'It's me,' Pippa said.

'Oh, hi. Sorry, Pippa,' I giggled. 'There's been Bimbos on the line all morning.'

'There still is,' Amanda said. 'And don't call my friends *Bimbos*!'

'I got the Blowbubble pack this morning,' Pippa said. 'I wondered if you'd like to come over and help me fill out the form?'

'You didn't tell me you called up for an application!' I said. 'The whole *world's* gone bubble gum crazy.'

'Andy and Fern are coming over,' Pippa said. 'Andy says he wants to be my manager, and Fern says she's going to groom me for success.'

I couldn't help laughing at that.

'I guess you *do* need me,' I said. 'I'll be right over.'

Amanda was writing with her tongue out. I'd noticed before that the more Amanda tried to concentrate, the further out she stuck her tongue. Right then, her tongue was clear across the room and hanging in the sink, so I guess she was concentrating real hard.

I leaned over her shoulder.

' "I think I should be chosen as the Blowbubble face of the year," ' I read aloud, ' "because." Because? Because what?'

'I can't decide what to put first,' Amanda mumbled.

'Uh, how about: because America's biggest bubble gum company deserves to be promoted by Four Corners' biggest bubblehead,' I suggested.

'Get lost!'

The doorbell rang. Boy, this was one busy morning for the bells in our house.

'I'll get it on my way out,' I said. I called to tell Mom I was going to Pippa's house, and then I opened the front door.

A crazy carrot-haired stick-insect came flying through the door, waving a bunch of papers.

'These arrived this morning,' Rachel babbled, running straight past me and bounding up the stairs two at a time. 'Amanda! Amanda!' she hollered. 'I got it! I got it!'

'She's in the kitchen,' I called up to her. Rachel nearly fell on her face as she slammed on the brakes at the top of the stairs and came racing back down.

I closed the door behind me.

I was right: the whole darned world *had* gone completely and utterly bubble gum crazy!

Chapter Four

'OK, Fern,' Andy said. 'Walk and stop and turn and smile.'

Fern did a bow-legged cowboy-walk across the floor, stopped, turned and pulled a seriously bad face at the three of us sitting on Pippa's bed.

'Chew Blowbubble Bubble Gum and you'll never have to brush your teeth again,' she said in a TV-ad kind of voice. ''Cos they'll all fall out! *Da-daa*!'

Andy looked at Pippa. 'And that is why Fern is not entering for the tryouts.'

'I could do it just fine if I felt like it,' Fern said as she threw herself on the floor. 'But I'm not a total dork.'

'There's nothing *dorky* about it,' Pippa said. 'We intelligent people have got to make a stand against the, uh, tide of mediocrity that's sweeping the nation.'

We all stared at her.

'Huh?' I said.

Pippa shrugged. 'Some guy on TV said it in a programme my mom was watching the other day.'

'Was it a cartoon?' Andy asked.

'No, it was not!' Pippa said. 'My mom doesn't watch— oh! Well, ha, ha, Andy, big joke!' She frowned. 'The point is that you guys should be encouraging me,' she glared at Fern, 'not calling me a dork.'

'OK,' I said. 'I guess *someone* has to stand against Amanda and the Bimbos. I mean, can you imagine what life would be like if one of them actually *won*?'

LIFE WITH AMANDA IF SHE WON

(Amanda is lying on her enormous pink heart-shaped bed. She is wearing a pink, silk robe. Stacy, wearing rags, is applying pink polish to Amanda's toenails.)

Amanda: Stacy, I'm feeling really tired. Yawn for me, will you, please, I can't be bothered.

Stacy: Sure thing, Amanda. (Yawns)

Amanda: Oh, and I'm getting kind of thirsty. Bring me an orange juice — and *pronto*!

Stacy: One orange-juice-and-pronto coming up, Amanda.

Amanda: And then you can take a break, Stacy. You've earned it. Once you've fed me some fresh-peeled grapes, cleaned my room, brought me my magazines, run me a bubble bath, done my homework, answered my fan-mail, worshipped at my feet for a while, polished all my mirrors, told me how great I am and carried me to the solarium so I can work on my tan.

Of course, I could be *wrong*. I mean, life with Amanda might be *worse* than that.

'The way I see it, guys,' Pippa said, 'most of the people who enter for the tryouts are going to be relying on good looks.' She pointed to herself. 'I, on the other hand, am going to deliver a *total package*. Looks, charm and intelligence.'

Fern shook her head. 'I'm not too sure about the looks,' she said.

'I wish you wouldn't keep going *on* about the way I look, Fern!' Pippa said. 'Anyone would think I was utterly hideous.'

She stared hard at each of us in turn. There was a lo-o-o-ong silence.

'I said,' Pippa said very slowly and clearly, '*anyone would think I was utterly hid*— oh, forget it!'

'Listen,' Fern said, 'you're not *utterly* hideous, Pippa.'

'You're just not, uh, *glamorous*,' I said. 'You're kind of ordinary looking.'

'And if girls like Amanda and Natalie are going to enter the competition,' Andy said, 'then ordinary-looking people are going to get blown clean out of the water.' He smiled encouragingly. 'We're only telling you this for your own good.'

'You guys are *not* listening to me!' Pippa said. 'OK, I know I'm not *perfect* looking. That's the whole point! I'm making a stand for all us ordinary-looking people with *brains*. Get it? Why should all our role models be bimbos like Natalie?' Pippa stood up. 'It's time that bubble gum was advertised by someone who knows the capital of Maryland! By someone who can quote the average rainfall in Iowa! By someone who can spell Mississippi!'

'You mean by a *nerd*?' Fern asked.

Pippa slumped onto the floor like a pricked balloon.

'Hey, don't worry,' I said, patting her shoulder comfortingly. 'Some real nice people are nerds.'

'I think Pippa's right,' Andy said. 'And I think we should give her our total support.'

'Hold the train,' Fern said. 'Even if we do think brains are important, how come everyone is assuming that *Pippa* is the obvious choice? There are other people around here with *brains*.'

'That's nice of you to say, Fern,' I said. 'But I don't really want to become a household name.'

'Huh!' Fern snorted. 'Some joke!'

'I think I'm probably just a *little* smarter than you, Fern,' I said as politely as I could. 'I mean, let's not forget which of us Super-glued her bottom to a chair and had to be carried, sitting down, to the hospital to get unstuck.'

'That was *ages* ago!' Fern said.

'That was last year!' I said.

'*Wait a minute!*' Fern exclaimed. 'Who put the tube of Superglue on the chair in the first place, huh? *You* did, Stacy.'

'So you had to *sit* on it?' I yelled. 'You should take more care of where you put your big behind!'

'I do not have a big behind!' Fern hollered. 'And at least my teeth grow straight!' She held her hands up to her mouth with her fingers splayed all over, like some kind of nightmare tooth-explosion.

'Quiet!' Pippa shouted. She looked crossly at us. 'Way to decide whose got the best *brain*, guys!' she said. 'And, anyway, it's not just brains. It's personality, too.'

'So, I win again!' Fern said.

'You do not!' I said.

'Why don't you two go sign up for the competition?' Andy suggested.

'What?' I said. 'Just to prove something that everyone already knows? That I'm smarter and more *charis-thingy* than Fern.'

'The word is *charismatic*,' Fern said smugly. 'And you *aren't*!'

'Am, too!'

'Are not!'

'Am, too, doubled!'

'Are not, *tripled*!'

'Am, too, quadrupled and no return! *Nyahhh*!'

I decided the best thing was to ignore Fern. She can be so childish sometimes!

'Pippa,' I said in a really dignified and calm way, 'would you like to ask Fern if she's prepared to put her money where her mouth is and enter the competition?'

'Tell Stacy that I'd be delighted to enter,' Fern said. 'In fact, if I may use your phone, Pippa, I'll call up for an entry form right now.'

'Me, too,' I said. 'And may the best girl win!'

'That's real kind of you, Stacy,' Fern said.

'Guys?' Pippa wailed, 'What about me? I asked you over to help *me*.'

'No problem,' Andy said cheerfully. 'I'll help you.' He grinned around at us. 'In fact, I'm going to help the whole bunch of you! How does *that* sound?'

Pippa shook her head. 'Doom!' she said.

Chapter Five

'What are you doing, Stacy?'

Amanda's voice came out of *nowhere*. I nearly jumped right out of my underwear with the shock. The photographs I'd been looking through went everywhere.

'Don't creep up on people like that!' I gasped.

'What are you so uptight about?' Amanda asked, crouching down next to where I was sitting. 'Doing something sneaky, huh?'

'No!'

I was sitting on the floor in front of the cabinet in our living room. I had the bottom drawer open and I'd been going through old picture albums.

I wasn't doing it *sneakily*, though. I just didn't want Amanda to know. Because if Amanda saw me going through old family pictures, Amanda would ask why. And if I told her the truth, she'd laugh her stupid *head* off!

I was looking for a picture to send back

with my filled-in application form. Yeah, I'd phoned in for one. So had Fern, even though the two of us soon got over our argument. In the end we just did it for fun.

I hadn't found anything I liked in the albums, and I was looking through the more recent pictures that Mom hadn't gotten around to sticking in. I guess most families have a heap of pictures like that — ones that haven't been put in albums yet.

That was when Amanda had turned up.

I scrabbled around on the carpet, gathering the pictures together again.

'So how come you're behaving like you're doing something sneaky?' Amanda asked. She picked up a couple of pictures of baby Sam. Sam was born last year. Mom said he was a *happy accident*, which meant his arrival wasn't exactly *planned* down to the last detail, if you know what I mean. But it also meant everyone was really pleased and excited when he *did* come, even though he took over the entire house in about ten seconds flat.

Anyway, Sam featured in about ninety per cent of all the recent pictures. Sam in his car-rycot. Sam in his crib. Sam lying in my lap. Sam lying in Amanda's lap. Sam in the bathtub. Sam being burped by Dad. Sam being fed by Gran. Sam struggling to get loose from Aunt Susie.

'These are dynamite, Stacy,' Amanda said as she went through the pictures. 'When he's older, we're going to have so much *fun* with these!'

'How?'

'Oh, you know, we can show them to his buddies when he's trying to be cool,' Amanda said with a big grin. 'Or take them out when he invites girlfriends home. The usual things.'

'That's pretty mean.'

'Listen, shortstuff, big sisters have a *duty* to humiliate their little brothers when they bring girlfriends home,' Amanda said. 'You may not like it, but I'm afraid it's just one of those things you've *got* to do.'

And then the thing I'd been dreading finally happened.

As she put the baby pictures she'd been looking at onto the pile I'd gathered in my lap, she glanced down and saw the application form on the floor.

'What's *this*?' she asked, grabbing it before I had the chance to stop her.

'Nothing,' I yelled. 'Gimme it back!'

She fended me off with one arm.

'Hah!' she crowed. 'I *thought* so! No wonder you've raced to get to the mail first every day!

Expecting a letter from Cindy, huh? You were waiting for *this*!'

'What if I was?' I said, desperately trying to retrieve the entry form before Amanda had the chance to start reading my responses.

'You've been making fun of me and my friends for the past *two weeks* about this,' Amanda yelled. 'And all the time you were getting a form of your own. Of all the two-faced people, Stacy! So that's what you're doing. You're looking for a picture to send off! And I caught you! Ha!'

'I can try for it if I want,' I said. 'It's a free country. I don't have to ask your permission.'

'No, but you could have asked my *advice*,' Amanda said, still holding me off with one hand as I tried to get the form back. 'And I would have advised you to stop before you started.'

'How can someone stop *before* they've started?' I said.

'With a face like yours, it's easy.'

I gave Amanda a hefty shove. 'I hate you!' I yelled.

Amanda looked startled. 'Hey, hey,' she said. 'I was only kidding.'

'No you weren't. You think I'm ugly.'

'You're not ugly,' Amanda said. She grinned. 'Well, maybe just a *little* ugly.' She laughed. 'But if you put a sack over your head, you might stand a chance.' She had hold of my wrist so I couldn't get away.

'Now then,' she said. 'Let's see what you've written.'

She flipped the top page over with one hand.

' "I should be the face of Blowbubble Bubble Gum," ' she started reading, ' "because I think people are sick and tired of looking at all those PERFECT people who always get chosen to appear in commercials. It's about time someone was chosen who looks like a regular everyday person. Then people who see the advertisements will think, *Hey, that looks just like me; I think I'll go buy a pack of Blowbubble Bubble Gum.* That's my opinion, anyway. And smart people are more interesting to look at than dumb people." '

'Go on!' I yelled. 'Have a good laugh.'

'No way, Stacy,' Amanda said. 'I like it. I really do.'

I stopped struggling. 'You do?'

'Sure,' Amanda said. 'It's . . . uh, *different.*'

I stared at her. 'You really think it's OK?' I asked. 'Do you think they'll go for it?'

Amanda shrugged. 'I wouldn't go *that* far, Stacy,' she said. 'They'll probably think you're some kind of nut.'

'Thanks!'

'Face it, Stacy,' Amanda said in her most irritating I'm-older-than-you-so-I-know-everything voice. 'You can only take the plain-but-interesting approach so far. In the end they're going to want someone with good looks and a great personality. If you don't have those, then you could be some kind of mega-genius, but you're not going to wind up on TV selling bubble gum.'

'Pippa thinks they want someone ordinary looking,' I said. 'They don't mention *anywhere* that you have to be super-gorgeous or anything.'

'Pippa would think that,' Amanda said. 'She's weirder looking than you!'

'She is?'

'By a *mile*!' Amanda said.

I know this will sound terrible, but I felt quite pleased about that. It was the closest thing to a compliment Amanda had ever come out with. I mean, I'd never *tell* Pippa what Amanda had said, but it was kind of comforting to know Amanda didn't think I was the homeliest kid in town!

'So, you think I should send in the form?' I asked.

'Why not?' Amanda said. 'Just don't be too disappointed when you don't get called for the tryouts.'

'Who says I won't?'

'They'll be looking for something special,' Amanda said with a toss of her head. 'Something just that little bit *extra*. That's why I'm going to win.'

'What do *you* have that's so darned special?' I asked.

'Stacy,' Amanda said, 'there's such a thing as star quality. I can't help it if I was born with it and you weren't!'

'Oh yeah?' I snapped. 'We'll see about that!'

Amanda laughed. 'And what's *that* supposed to mean?'

'It means you're not going to win!' I said. 'I am!'

Me and my big mouth! Why do I let myself be bothered by my airhead sister? Now we were competing against each other. Which meant that if Amanda *did* win, I would never, ever hear the end of it!

Amanda stood up. She patted me on the head in the way that she *knew* drove me crazy.

'Dream on, Stacy,' she said. 'You have as much chance of being the Blowbubble face of the year as you have of winning the lottery!'

'But we don't play the lottery,' I said.

'Exactly!' Amanda said as she flounced out of the room. 'Now, excuse me while I go prepare my winner's speech.'

I could still hear her as she went up the stairs. 'I'd just like to thank all my friends and family,' she burbled in a totally fake-sounding voice, 'I'd never have won without their encouragement and support. And I'd just like to say to all those people who've written to me, that my secretary will be replying personally to each and every one of you, and that I love you all!'

Blecch! My sister the superstar! I sure hope *not!*

But meanwhile, I still had a halfway-decent picture of myself to find. One thing was for sure, I couldn't back out of entering the contest now.

And there was still the chance that Amanda might not get picked.

Or so I *hoped*, until a letter arrived for Amanda a week later, from the office of Thelonius P Appleby, informing her that it was his *'great pleasure to invite Amanda Allen to the preliminary competition round, to be held in the Grosvenor Sports Centre in Four Corners'* on the following Saturday.

'Like I said,' Amanda crowed, waving the letter under my nose. 'Some people are born with star quality, and some aren't.'

Chapter Six

It was Friday. Not just *any* Friday. It was the Friday before the Saturday of the Blowbubble Bubble Gum tryouts. I sat on the stairs all morning waiting for the mail to be delivered.

The thing was, that I still hadn't heard back from Thelonius P Appleby. I'd managed to find a halfway-decent picture of myself where my freckles weren't too obvious.

It seemed like everyone except for Fern and me had been invited to the tryouts on Saturday. All the Bimbos were going to be there. Even Pippa had received her invitation. And it seemed like everyone in town was practising bubble-blowing. It was the latest craze.

I knew Fern and I had left it a little late with our application forms, but you'd think the Blowbubble people would make an effort to reply to everyone in time.

After I'd been sitting there blowing bubble gum bubbles and staring at the front door for about twenty million years, the mailman finally pulled up outside the house. I raced outside before he could put the letters in our mailbox.

Two bills for Dad. A letter for Mom. One of those multi-coloured free-offer-type envelopes addressed to someone called Mrs Boobera Alien and telling her she'd already won a *very special prize* which was waiting for her if she replied within ten days.

But nothing for me.

'Rats! Rats! Rats!' I yelled.

Amanda's head appeared around the kitchen door. 'Is that three different rats?' she asked. 'Or the same rat three times?'

'It still hasn't come!' I said. 'What's the matter with the mail these days?'

James's head popped out beside Amanda's. 'When did you send it off, Stacy?'

'Just before the deadline,' Amanda said. 'It's hardly surprising there's nothing back, yet.'

'What am I going to do?' I said. 'By the time I get the letter telling me to go to the tryouts it'll be too late!'

'Call them,' Amanda said decisively. 'Tell them you haven't heard anything and you need to know if you should show up at the tryouts.'

'Hey, I *could* do that,' I said, feeling suddenly a whole lot better. 'Thanks, Amanda.'

I borrowed Amanda's acceptance letter for

the phone number. That same cheerful voice thanked me for calling and told me to hold the line. Then there was about five minutes of really gruesome music, like you get in elevators.

Suddenly there was a click and a familiar voice spoke over the music.

'Who's that?' it asked.

'My name's Stacy Allen,' I said. 'I was just—'

'Stacy? I need to make a call, honey.' No wonder it was a familiar voice! It was Mom! She'd picked up the extension in her office in the basement.

Over the next two hours I tried Blowbubble's head office a whole bunch of times, but I never got any further than the horrible music and the voice telling me my call would be answered soon. Except that it never was!

'Mom will go crazy when she gets the phone bill,' Amanda told me after she'd finished showing off to James by blowing a bubble bigger than her head. 'Twenty calls to Chicago in one morning!' I was sitting out on the patio with Amanda and James between phone-runs.

'I don't see why,' I said. 'It's not like I've *spoken* to anyone.'

'You get charged from the moment you get connected, Stacy,' Amanda said, peering at me over her sunglasses. 'It doesn't matter if you speak to anyone or not.'

'Get out of here,' I said.

'It's true,' James said. 'All the time you're hanging on, you're being charged for the call.'

Oops! I decided maybe I'd better quit trying to get through to Blowbubble's head office.

'Maybe they'll call you,' Amanda said as she stretched out on her towel to soak up some sun. She yawned. 'Maybe they saw your late application and realized you were *the one*, and now they're going crazy up there trying to contact you before tomorrow.' She chewed for a few seconds then started to blow another bubble.

I was just giving Amanda a withering look when the phone rang.

Amanda expertly deflated her bubble. 'There they are now,' she said.

Yeah, sure!

It was Fern.

'Well?' she said. 'Have you?'

'Have I, what?'

'Oh, come on! You must have!' She sounded excited.

'What are you talking about, Fern?'

'You mean you *haven't*?'

'I'm not in the mood for this,' I said. 'What the heck do you want?'

'I got the letter this morning,' Fern shrieked. 'I'm sitting here with it in my hand *right now*! They want me to go along to the tryouts tomorrow!' There was a pause. 'Uh, didn't you get a letter?'

'Not yet,' I said gloomily.

'Oh.' There was another pause. I hoped maybe Fern was trying to think up something comforting to say. 'Hey,' she said after a few moments, 'maybe they don't bother sending letters to all the losers, huh?'

'Well, thank *you*!' I yelled.

'Sheesh!' Fern said. 'You could be pleased for *me*, Stacy.'

'Yeah,' I said, 'I'm, like, *totally* pleased for you. I'm so *happy* that you and Pippa got accepted that I think I'm just going to have to hang up now and go sing on the roof, Fern!'

There was a short pause. 'You don't really mean that, Stacy,' Fern said. 'I can tell. Look, don't sweat it. There's still tomorrow.'

I guess she was right. At least I had that one tiny shred of hope left. To be honest, I couldn't have cared less about *winning* the darned thing, but it was kind of annoying to be the only person not even to be invited to the tryouts!

I wandered out into the garden.

'That was Fern,' I told Amanda and James.

'She's going to the tryouts, too,' I said. 'Isn't that *great*?'

James gave me a sympathetic look.

'Hey, Amanda and I are going ice skating this afternoon,' he said. 'You can come with us.'

Amanda gave him such a look!

'Are you *sure*?' I said. Amanda likes to keep James pretty much to herself most of the time.

'Sure!' James said with a smile.

'Amanda?' I asked. 'Is that OK?'

She looked at James. 'Why not?' she said with a shrug. 'I guess you could use cheering up, Stacy.' She stretched and sat up. 'It must be time for another skating lesson by now, anyhow. What are we up to, Stacy — lesson number six zillion and four, isn't it?'

'Don't exaggerate,' I said. 'It's only six zillion and *two*.'

★ ★ ★

The thing with me and ice skating is that I can do *some* things really well, but I have real trouble with *other* things.

Like, I can lace up the skates *perfectly*. And I can zoom along *forwards* just fine so long as it's not too fast, and so long as there's someone nearby to hang onto if anything goes wrong.

But when it comes to stopping or making

54

neat turns or going *backwards*, then I kind of go all to pieces and wind up on my backside on the ice.

Amanda says I have a permanent *mental block*. James just says I need to practise more. I prefer James's opinion. James is utterly brilliant on the ice. He's better than Amanda, and Amanda is pretty darned good.

Our local ice rink is called *Paradice*. An hour later that afternoon, the three of us had put our hired skates on and we were heading out onto the ice.

I wobbled around on my own for a few minutes while Amanda and James did some speed-work together. Amanda likes to start a session by whizzing around really fast a few times. She calls it *warming up*, but I'd call it *showing off*, if I wasn't being so polite.

Then it was my turn. James took hold of my hand and we went whooshing around the rink together. He made it look so easy. And he made me feel really *safe*. With James as my partner, I almost felt like a professional!

And now, out on the ice, the stunning new partnership of James Baker and Stacy Allen. This couple have been wowing audiences all the way from New York to San Francisco. They have the style, the grace, and they sure know how to inter-

*pret the music! This thrilling young couple is really
going places, folks. And now James whirls Stacy
around in a dog-leg double-axel backflip, followed
by Stacy's brilliant single-lutz off-the-wall toespin
leading into the famous simultaneous triple somer-
sault and the patented Allen punch-jump. They're
pulling out all the stops this afternoon, folks, and
the audience is showing its appreciation in the
usual way!*

'Hey! Freak-face! Clear the road!'
   Thump! Whack! Splat!
   I was *punch-jumped* right out of my day-
dream as some big idiot came crunching into
me and knocked me onto my *tail* on the ice.
   'Careful!' I heard James shout.
   'She should keep out of my way!' I recognized the voice. It was Judy MacWilliams.
   Judy MacWilliams goes to the same school
as Amanda and me. She's in Amanda's grade
and they absolutely *hate* each other. I mean,
honestly, I can't *tell* you how much they loathe,
detest and hate the sight of each other.
   The problem is that they're total rivals in
just about everything. Like, when Amanda
was picked as head cheerleader instead of
Judy, the first thing Judy did was to quit the
squad. And more recently, Judy was respons-
ible for James and Amanda almost splitting

56

up. She'd do *anything* to annoy or upset Amanda. And, to be honest, I'm pretty sure Amanda feels the same right back at her.

So, there she was, standing there with her long black hair and her fringe down to her eyes, glaring down at me with her fists on her hips, dressed in the tightest leotard you've ever seen. Like, you couldn't just *count* her ribs through it, you could play a xylophone solo on them!

'Ouch!' I said, glaring up at her. 'You clumsy elephant! Why don't you watch where you're going?'

'Get lost!' Judy said. 'You had your eyes closed!'

James helped me to my feet just as Amanda came skimming over.

'What's going on?' she asked. 'I saw you— oh!' She spotted Judy. 'It's *you*! I should have known!'

Judy gave her a sneery look. 'Tell your little sister she should look where she's going, otherwise someone is gonna run right over her.'

'Just try it,' Amanda snarled.

'Oh, I'm so scared!' Judy sneered. 'Look at me, I'm trembling all over!'

'Forget it, Amanda,' James said. 'She's not worth it.'

'That's right,' Judy sniggered. 'Do what James tells you, Amanda, like the good little loser you are.'

'Loser? Huh!' Amanda said. 'The only loser I can see around here is *you*!'

Judy came back with a long, slow grin. 'Is that so?' she drawled. 'Well, we'll just see about that tomorrow.'

Amanda frowned at her. 'Oh, right,' she said. 'So you're in the competition, too?'

'Correction,' Judy said. 'I'm going to *win* the competition.'

'I don't think so,' Amanda said.

'Oh, I think I will,' Judy retorted. 'In fact, I'm so certain that I'm gonna win that I'm prepared to have a little side-bet with you, Amanda. If you've got the *guts* that is.'

'Name it,' Amanda said.

'OK. Let's make it something interesting. How about, when I win, you agree to quit as head cheerleader.'

'Fine!' Amanda snapped. 'In fact, if you win, Judy, I'll quit the squad! And when *I* win, *you* have to announce over the school PA system to the entire school that you're a total drongo!'

A great big smile stretched right across Judy's face.

'Deal!' she said. She looked at James and

me. 'And you two are witnesses.' She laughed. 'I am going to enjoy this so much!'

Her cheeks ballooned out as she started to blow a bubble gum bubble. Then she skated off while the bubble grew and grew. Trust Judy to be an expert with bubble gum. I kind of hoped the bubble would explode in her face, but it didn't.

'Amanda?' James said quietly. 'Was that such a good idea?'

'Excuse me,' Amanda said. 'Are you suggesting for one *minute* that Judy has the slightest chance of beating *me*?'

'Uh, no.'

'Does she have a better personality than me?'

'Not at all!'

'Is she better looking than me?'

'No way!'

Amanda stared at James. 'So? What's the problem?'

James held his hands up. 'No problem,' he said.

But I wasn't so sure. OK, so Judy and Amanda were always at each other's throats. But there was something about the way Judy had behaved just then. Something more than her usual boasting. If anyone asked me, I'd

say Judy had behaved like she *knew* she was
going to win.

Except that she *couldn't* know. Could she?

Chapter Seven

'*Whooo-hoooo!*' I yelled. '*Wahhheyyyyy!*' I waved the letter in the air and did a quick dance around the hall.

Dad came out of the kitchen with Sam tucked under one arm.

'Did you get some mail?' Dad asked.

'IT!' I hollered. '*IT!*'

I ran halfway up the stairs and yelled in the general direction of Amanda's room. 'It arrived! It *arrived*!'

Amanda came out and leaned over the banisters.

'What are you yelling about?'

'My letter,' I shouted. 'They want me at the competition!'

Amanda tossed her hair and headed back to her room. 'Thank heavens for that,' she said. 'Now I don't have to be all sympathetic any more!'

'There's a letter for you, too,' I said to Dad.

'It's probably a bill,' he said. 'Leave it on the kitchen table for me, honeybunch.'

'Sure thing,' I said. I gave Sam a big kiss on his fluffy blonde hair then ran into the kitchen to show my letter to Mom.

I smoothed it out flat on the table in front of her and started reading it aloud.

'Stacy,' Mom said quietly. 'I *can* read.'

'Yeah,' I said, 'but look, it says, "The preliminary tryouts will be taking place in the Grosvenor Sports Centre at 2pm on Saturday the twenty ninth." That's *today*!'

'I already know all this,' Mom said. 'Amanda's been talking about nothing else for two weeks, and you haven't exactly been totally silent on the subject.'

'Yeah, but look: "We feel certain from your application form that you are exactly the type of young person Blowbubble Bubble Gum would choose to be the face of this year's advertising campaign. Therefore we have great pleasure in inviting you to attend the tryouts." ' I grinned at Mom. 'Did you read that?' I said. 'I'm exactly the type of person they want.'

'Amanda's letter said the same thing,' Mom said. 'In fact, these are duplicated letters, honey. I expect everyone got exactly the same thing.'

'But it has my name printed on it,' I said.

'Trust me,' Mom said. 'It's done on a machine.'

Dad leaned over me to look.

'I don't think that matters,' he said. 'The point is that Stacy has been asked to go to the tryouts.'

Mom gave him an expressive look. 'David,' she said, (she only calls him *David* in that tone of voice when she's a little irritated about something), 'Everyone who applied will have been accepted. This whole thing is one big *hype* intended to sell more bubble gum.'

Amanda came strolling in. 'Aw, Mom,' she said, 'don't be such a party pooper. It's just *fun*. OK? No one's taking it seriously.'

Huh! I thought. *You'll be taking it seriously enough if Judy wins.*

Mom stood up. 'I won't say another word about it,' she said. 'I can't get a sensible word out of either of my daughters these days because they've always got bubble gum in their mouths. Well, don't expect me to join in, that's all!' She opened the basement door and marched down to her office.

'Take no notice of your mom,' Dad said with a smile. 'She's stressed out with work right now.'

'I heard that!' Mom yelled. 'And I am not!'

63

'What's with Mom?' Amanda asked. 'Anyone would think we were planning on dancing topless on national television.'

Dad sat down and picked up his letter.

He frowned. 'It's from the office,' he said. 'That's strange.' He jammed his thumb under the flap.

'Dad?' Amanda persisted. 'What's Mom's problem with this bubble gum thing?'

'I don't think she has a problem with it, honey,' Dad said. 'The people she works for are pressuring her to take more on, and it's getting her down. Don't worry about it, she'll be as pleased as I will if you win.'

'Excuse me?' I said. 'If *who* wins?'

Dad laughed. 'Either of you,' he said. 'You're both as cute as two bugs in a bedsheet.'

'How cute is *that*?' I asked. Two bugs in a bedsheet didn't sound cute to me at *all*.

Dad didn't answer. He sat staring at the single sheet of paper that he'd pulled out of the envelope.

'I guess you *do* stand a chance,' Amanda said, giving me the once-over with a calculating look on her face. 'It depends on whether they go for the pedigree look or the mutt look.'

'What does that mean?'

'It's like in a dog show,' Amanda said. 'They sometimes give a prize to some dopey-looking

64

pooch just for a change.' She grinned. 'Get the picture, poochie?'

'Dad!'

'Not now, sweetie,' Dad said. He stood up and walked out of the kitchen with the letter in his hand and a really worried look on his face.

'What do you think it was?' I breathed to Amanda.

'Beats me,' she said. 'But I'll tell you something, I don't think it was good news.' She stood up. 'Anyway, I don't have time to sit here talking to you, Stacy. I've got things to do.'

'Yeah,' I said. 'Like making sure you've got a wet *nose* and a glossy *coat*, Lassie.'

'I didn't hear that, Stacy,' Amanda called from the stairs. 'Could you *bark* a little louder?'

Chapter Eight

'Excuse me! Coming through! Excuse me! Thank you!' Amanda elbowed her way through the crowd in the foyer of the Grosvenor Sports Centre. I followed along in her wake.

It seemed like everyone in Four Corners between the ages of five and fifteen was crammed in there. And the younger ones were with their parents. Everyone was fighting for their tiny piece of space and everyone was yelling at the tops of their voices when they weren't blowing wobbly pink bubbles.

Amanda had spent most of the morning in the bathroom, and when she wasn't in there she was calling the Bimbos on the phone to check that they weren't going to all wear the same clothes to the tryouts.

I'd arranged to meet my friends in the foyer of the sports centre.

Some chance! It was packed solid.

Everyone was dressed really well. There

were quite a few boys around and all the older girls were wearing make-up — including Amanda.

And me? I'd decided I may as well go for the cute girl-next-door look. I mean, let's be honest here, there was no point in me trying to look glamorous. I would have to win the judges over with my *personality*. If I could come across as honest, hard-working, genuine, friendly, cheerful and loveable, then I might stand a chance. The trouble was that the way my stomach was feeling right then, I was more likely to come across as tongue-tied, nervous, shaky and nerdy.

I hadn't expected to feel so anxious.

The Stacy-angel: Hey, chill out, Stacy. It's only a tryout for some dumb bubble gum commercial. No problemo! You'll walk it.

The Stacy-demon: Yeah, and when you walk it, you're going to trip up and fall on your face, Stacy. Then you're going to stand there in front of all those people and you're not going to be able to say a WORD. And then your underpants will fall down! Humiliation-city, Stacy!

'Hey, Stacy! Over here!' Pippa's voice came from over to the left. I stood right up on tiptoes.

I saw her and Andy over by the snack machines under the stairs. They were both waving.

I abandoned Amanda and squidged and squodged my way through to my friends.

Pippa was wearing her very best clothes. Not her best *party* clothes, but her best going-to-a-classical-music-concert-with-her-mom clothes. And she had her hair pulled back even tighter and smoother than normal. And she was wearing a pair of glasses that were way too big for her.

I stared at her. 'Why?' I said.

'Why what?'

'The glasses, Pippa. You don't need glasses.'

'They were Andy's idea,' Pippa said.

'I decided Pippa should go for the child-prodigy, super-genius effect,' Andy said. 'The glasses make her look smart.'

'Smart-*er*,' Pippa said. She had a book in her hand. A very thick book. She held it up for me to see.

' "*Moby Dick*," ' I read, ' "by Herman Melville." ' I blinked at her. 'Is it any good?'

'It sure is,' Pippa said. 'It's the story of a man's metaphysical quest for the devil inside himself, as personified by a great white whale.'

I nodded. 'Yeah,' I said, 'I thought it would

68

be something like that. Sometimes I think you forget what a total weirdo you are, Pippa.'

'Speaking of weirdos,' Andy said, 'here's Fern.'

Fern hadn't gone for the cute girl-next-door type.

She hadn't gone for the super-genius type either.

So far as I could tell, she'd gone for the whacked-out cyber-punk totally-off-her-head crazy-girl look. She had on clothes that looked like they'd been caught in a shredder and then sewn back together by a colour-blind chimpanzee. Her hair had been back-combed so that it stood up in spikes all over her head. She had on sunglasses and a red headband. And she was wearing enormous black boots.

'Hi, guys,' she said.

'Have your folks seen you like that?' Pippa asked.

'They sure have,' Fern grinned. 'Dad lent me the psychedelic vest and Mom fixed my hair for me. What do you think?'

'It's different,' I said.

'Very different,' Pippa agreed.

'*Extremely* different,' Andy added.

Fern grinned. '*Totally* different,' she said. 'That was the whole point. I wanted to stand out from the crowd.'

'You certainly do that,' I said.

'OK, everyone! Listen up!' a man's voice yelled above the noise. We turned to look up at the balcony where the man and about half a dozen other people were standing holding clipboards.

'Quiet down, please!' the man called. He clapped his hands. 'Hey! The quicker I get your complete attention, the quicker we can get this show on the road.' The last few murmurings stopped.

'Thank you,' the man said. 'My name is Ed Munrow, and I'm overall head of the Blow-bubble Bubble Gum marketing department. Which means I'm in charge of today's event.'

'Where's Thelonius Appleby?' a voice yelled from somewhere.

'He's not here today,' Ed Munrow said. 'But I can tell you guys, he'd be really pleased at such a terrific turn out. And I can promise he'll be here next week when the lucky finalists will be invited back for decision time.'

'I thought they were going to decide *today*,' Fern said quietly. 'What's all this about *next week*?'

'Didn't you read the letter?' Pippa said. 'These are just the *preliminary* tryouts.'

'Let's try and keep together, huh?' I whispered to Pippa and Fern. I thought I'd feel less nervous if I had my friends with me.

They nodded.

'OK,' Ed Munrow said. 'I'd like to start off by welcoming you all on behalf of Thelonius P Appleby and Blowbubble Bubble Gum. We all hope you have a really great time today. First off, I'd like to introduce you to the team who'll be working with you this afternoon.' One by one the other people up on the gallery stepped forwards and smiled as Ed Munrow told us their names.

'Now,' Ed Munrow said, 'as there are so many of you, we're going to have to split you up into smaller groups. We're going to do this alphabetically by the first letter of your last name, right?' He beckoned to one of the young women with the clipboards. 'Tiffany will be taking all those of you whose last names begin with the letter A through D, OK? So could everyone whose last name begins with A, B, C, or D, please meet up with Tiffany at the foot of the stairs, over there.' He pointed across the foyer from where I was standing.

'I guess I'll see you guys later,' I said. I looked at Pippa and Fern. 'You two will be together. Kipsak and Kane. And I've got to be with my sister. Oh, well, good luck, guys.'

'Yeah,' Pippa said. 'Good luck, Stacy.'

The last thing I heard as I pushed my way over to the far staircase was Fern saying, 'What's with the huge *glasses*, Pippa?'

I spotted Judy MacWilliams up near the front of the crowd. She was wearing skin-tight white jeans and she had a bare midriff. I stuck my tongue out at her even though she had her back to me.

About twenty of us gathered by the stairs. Tiffany led us up to the next floor and along a corridor.

She consulted her clipboard. 'We're in room B23,' she said. 'I have a map of the place here, but, I can't quite figure out where we are right now.'

'I know the room,' Amanda said. 'Follow me, guys.'

'Oh, thanks.' Tiffany said. To be honest, she seemed a little out of it. As we all walked along behind Amanda, Tiffany was constantly flicking through her papers as if she was still trying to figure out what was going on.

'Do you work in the Chicago office?' Amanda asked her. 'My dad's head office is in Chicago. He sells books.'

'Huh? Oh, no,' Tiffany said. 'I don't actually work for Blowbubble at all. I'm from a recruiting agency. I'm just doing this one job for them.' Her forehead wrinkled up. 'I think my papers are out of order.'

'I'd be happy to help sort them for you,' Amanda said. 'I guess you have a list of the kind of things you're looking for today, huh?' Amanda slowed down so she could peer at Tiffany's clipboard. 'The kind of personality points you're looking for?'

'Uh, no,' Tiffany said. 'Not really. It's not up to me.'

'What? Not at all?' Amanda asked. 'You mean you couldn't even put a word in for someone you thought had a really great personality and was very friendly and helpful?'

'There's a panel of judges,' Tiffany explained. 'It's up to them to decide.'

'Oh, right.'

Amanda must have realized she was wasting her time making nice to Tiffany. Still, it could have been worse for her: she might not have found out Tiffany couldn't put a word in for her until *after* she'd helped sort her papers.

'This is it!' Amanda said. 'Room B23.'

We all trooped in. I guessed the room was used for physiotherapy treatment or something like that. There was an adjustable couch and some other medical-type equipment.

There was a man waiting in there. He was

wearing jeans and a T-shirt and he had long hair tied back with a rubber band.

'OK, everyone,' Tiffany said, reading from her clipboard. 'This is Brad. You'll be working with him.'

'That's right,' Brad said. 'I'm going to ask you to come through one at a time.' He pointed to another door. 'All you need to do is look into a camera and read a simple message. It shouldn't take more than a minute per person.'

'And then what?' someone asked.

'And then you go home,' Tiffany said. 'And each of you will receive a free pack of Blow-bubble Bubble Gum.'

'You mean that's *it*?' Amanda said. 'I thought there'd be more to it than that.'

'The successful candidates will be called back to take part in the final tryouts next Saturday,' Tiffany said. 'That's when the big decision will be made. OK, everyone, let's get started.'

Tiffany handed a list of names to Brad. 'OK,' he said, 'Karen Abbot?'

A tall, skinny girl with buck teeth and frizzy hair followed him into the other room.

'Well, she's no competition,' Amanda whispered in my ear. She looked around. 'In fact,' she whispered, 'nobody here is all that great.'

74

A couple of minutes later Karen Abbot came out and Amanda was called.

'Wish me luck,' she said, walking into the other room like she was accepting her Academy Award.

Two minutes later Amanda came out. She winked at me.

'It's a cinch!' she said. 'You're next.'

I walked into the other room. It was plain white with no furniture or anything. In the middle of the floor Brad was bent over a video camera on a tripod, looking through the viewfinder. And behind him, on a frame, hung a big white board with writing on it.

'Stand on the blue cross,' Brad said without even looking at me. 'Read what's written on the board. And then smile into the camera.'

I cleared my throat and started to read.

' "Blowbubble Bubble Gum is the blubbiest" ... uh, sorry. That should be *bubbliest*. Sorry. It's kind of difficult.'

'That's OK,' Brad said, still only looking at me through the camera lens. 'Start again and just take your time.'

I cleared my throat. ' "Blowbubble Bubble Gum is the blubbliest glubble bum in" ... oh, heck!'

Finally Brad looked at me. 'Nervous?' he asked with a smile.

'A little, I guess,' I said.

Brad straightened up, jammed his fingers into the corners of his mouth and pulled his lips out sideways. Then he stuck his tongue out and went cross-eyed.

I was so surprised I just started laughing.

'That's it!' he said. 'Read it now!' He carried on pulling crazy faces while I tried to read from the board.

' "Blowbubble Bubble Gum is the bubbliest bubble gum in the whole wide world," ' I read, trying not to laugh. ' "And I love it!" '

'That was great,' Brad said. 'You're a star!'

'Really?'

I went out of that room feeling about ten feet tall.

Amanda was waiting for me in the hallway.

'Well?' she said. 'Did you do good?'

'Good?' I said. 'I did better than good! Brad told me I was a star.'

'Yeah, I bet!'

I just smiled at her. Amanda could believe what she liked. *I* knew what Brad had said. I was a *star*! Stacy the star.

Hey, know what? I was beginning to think that maybe I could *win* that competition. Now wouldn't that be something?

Chapter Nine

Back in the foyer a whole bunch of tables and stalls had been set up. It was like a Blowbubble merchandise store in there. You could buy T-shirts with the pink elephant logo on them. You could buy T-shirts that said 'I blew it at the Grosvenor — and I loved it!' You could buy key rings and lunch boxes and erasers and rulers and pens and pencils and badges and baseball caps and printed stationery. And there was a stall that sold different-flavoured Blowbubble Bubble Gum. There was even a table that sold cuddly, stuffed pink elephants with little Blowbubble vests and boxer shorts on and red balloons tied to the end of their trunks.

In fact, just about the only thing a person *couldn't* buy in there was a genuine pink elephant. And like Amanda said as we came down the stairs, they were probably working on *that*!

'I didn't bring any money,' I said, looking

at a big badge with a cartoon of the elephant with its trunk tied in a knot, saying, 'Don't forget to buy Blowbubble!'

The foyer was full of people running around like ants. The younger ones were dragging their parents from stall to stall and buying everything in sight. And nearly everyone was chewing or blowing bubbles or wiping exploded bubble gum off their faces.

I spotted Pippa and Fern. Fern had her mouth crammed with elephant-shaped candy but Pippa was just standing there looking annoyed.

'How did it go?' I asked them.

'*Murrghphlurghhh,*' Fern spluttered cheerfully.

'Terrible!' Pippa snapped. 'Don't ask!'

'Why? What happened?'

Pippa frowned at me. 'Did I just tell you not to ask, or what?' she said.

Fern swallowed. 'Pippa couldn't read the sign,' she said. 'That's why she's annoyed.'

'Dumb glasses!' Pippa said. 'And double dumb Andy for lending them to me in the first place.'

'You mean you couldn't *see* through them?' I said.

Pippa's forehead wrinkled. 'I could make out *shapes*,' she said. 'But everything was kind of blurry. I didn't know they were going to want me to *read* stuff.'

'Why didn't you just take them off?' I asked.

'Are you kidding?' Pippa said. 'They'd have thought I was a nut. What kind of a person has to take their glasses *off* to read?'

'I guess that would have looked a little strange,' I had to admit.

'And do you know something else?' Pippa said. 'I was talking to the guy who was looking after us, and he told me that every single person who sent in an application form got invited along here today. *Every single one!*'

Amanda came strolling over.

'There you go, Stacy,' she said, pinning a badge on me. 'Don't say I never buy you anything. Oh, and I'm going back to Cheryl's house, OK? Will you tell Mom?'

I looked down at the badge. It showed a tiny elephant blowing a bubble that looked like a red bubble gum version of the whole planet.

Amanda wandered off.

'I'm going to buy a T-shirt,' Fern said.

'Well, I'm going to find Andy,' Pippa said. 'And I'm going to stuff these glasses up his nose!'

★ ★ ★

79

'Mom! Dad!' I yelled the moment I got home. 'I'm a star! It's official!'

I ran into the living room. They were sitting on the couch together, holding hands and looking kind of serious.

'Hi, honey,' Mom said.

I skidded to a halt. 'What's wrong?' I asked.

'Nothing,' Dad said. 'Nothing for you to worry about.' He smiled. 'So, tell us all about it. Did you win?'

I crammed myself in between them on the couch and told them the whole story.

'And they're sending out letters to the finalists,' I finished. 'And Thelonius P Appleby himself is going to be on the panel of judges next week.'

Mom put her arm around me. 'I don't want you to be too disappointed if you're not a finalist, honey,' she said. 'This competition doesn't really *mean* anything, right? It's not *important*.'

'I know that,' I said. I grinned at her. 'But what if I *was* in the finals? Wouldn't that be something!'

'It sure would, honey,' Dad said. 'But what your mom means is, you shouldn't feel bad about yourself if you don't get chosen. We already *know* you're a star, whether some panel of judges realizes it or not.'

* * *

On Sunday we took a drive over to Gran and Grandad's for the day. Amanda and I told them all about the tryouts and Gran said that if the two of us didn't come joint first, then the judges had to be crazy.

We practised bubble blowing in front of Gran and Grandad until an especially *huge* bubble of mine exploded all over my sweater and Mom just about hit the roof.

'That will never come off!' she groaned, picking at the little bits of gum that were stuck all over the front of my sweater.

'I know how to get it off,' Gran said. She went into the kitchen and came back with some ice cubes.

She rubbed the ice cubes over the gum.

'You see?' she said. 'The cold makes the gum go hard, and then you can pick it off really easily.'

'How did you know that?' Amanda asked.

Gran smiled. 'Grans just *do*,' she said.

'Thank heavens they do,' Mom said. 'But no more bubbles! I've seen enough bubbles in the past two weeks to last a lifetime.'

Gran told us all about stuff she called 'deportment lessons'. *Deportment* is all to do with how you sit and stand and walk about.

'A refined young lady,' Gran told us, 'should be able to walk the length of a room and right up a flight of stairs with a book balanced on her head.' She smiled. 'And the book shouldn't even *wobble*.'

Amanda tried it with one of Grandad's big home improvement books on her head.

'Keep a straight back,' Gran explained. 'And try to walk as *smoothly* as you possibly can.'

'No problem,' Amanda said. She took about three steps before the book fell off.

'I know what the problem is,' I giggled. 'Amanda has a pointed head!'

'I'd like to see you do better!' Amanda said.

'I sure couldn't do any worse,' I said. Gran placed the book on my head. I took a careful step forwards. The book teetered.

'Keep your head up, Stacy,' Gran reminded me. 'And keep your back straight.'

'Yes. OK. I've got it,' I said. My eyes were nearly rolling right around in my head as I tried to keep watch on the front edge of the book. I spread my arms out like a tightrope walker and took another cautious step.

The book fell off.

'I think maybe you girls had better try this at home with some old books,' Mom said. And that was the end of our *deportment* lessons for the day.

* * *

On Monday the guys and I spent the day in Maynard Park with our dog, Lucky. Lucky lives with Fern, but he belongs to all of us. I don't really have time to explain *why* he belongs to all of us, he just *does*.

Lucky is only a puppy, but that didn't stop him from out-running the whole bunch of us and wearing us all out with games of 'toss the stick' and 'catch the ball'.

When I got home late in the afternoon, I was kind of half-hoping there would be a letter waiting for me. But there wasn't. The good thing was that there wasn't a letter waiting for Amanda either, which was a major relief. I didn't like to *think* how big-headed Amanda would get if she was picked for the finals and I wasn't.

* * *

The letters arrived Tuesday. Two letters. One for Amanda and one for me.

The two of us nearly tore the envelopes into little pieces right there in the hall.

My letter consisted of two sheets of paper

and a card with silver writing on it. It was an invitation card.

Thelonius P Appleby and the Blowbubble Corporation are pleased to invite STACY ALLEN to the finals of . . .

'*Waaaahh*! Mom!' Amanda shrieked right in my ear. 'I'm in the finals!'

'Me, too!' I hollered.

We danced around in the hall, hanging onto each other and screaming at the tops of our voices.

'We're in the finals! We're in the finals!' we yelled. I don't think I've ever been so excited by anything in my entire life!

Mom came up from the basement to check out the noise, but before she had a chance to say anything we were leaping all around her, waving our invitation cards in the air and shrieking with excitement.

'Calm down!' she hollered.

'But, *Mom*!'

'Yes, yes. It's great,' Mom laughed. 'I'm glad you're so happy. Just be happy a little more *quietly*, please. Sam's asleep down there.'

'I gotta call Cheryl,' Amanda babbled.

'I gotta call Pippa,' I said.

'Me first!' Amanda grabbed the phone.

Still laughing, Mom headed back down to

her office. Amanda sat on the stairs and punched out Cheryl's number.

I still couldn't really believe it. I sat on the floor and re-read my invitation card over and over.

I was in the *finals*! I had actually gotten into the finals of the competition to find the Blowbubble Bubble Gum face of the year! Wow! *Wow! WOW!*

Chapter Ten

Amanda and Cheryl shrieked at each other on the phone for about ten minutes. Anyone would think *I* didn't have people to call!

Cheryl's letter hadn't arrived.

'Amanda!' I said while Cheryl was doing some squawking from the other end. 'I need to call Pippa.'

'Yeah, sure thing,' Amanda said, waving me away. 'In a *minute*.'

I took a look at the two sheets of paper that had come with my invitation. One of them was headed *The Blowbubble Face of the Year Search!* and looked like a run-down of the things that would be going on next Saturday. The other page was headed *The Distinguished Panel of Judges*, and was just a list of names.

There was a note at the bottom of the page saying that nearly all the judges had been chosen from *distinguished residents* of Four Corners. The Chairman of the panel was a guy called Robert Dorian Phillips. I recognized a couple of the other names, and Thelonius P Appleby himself was one of the judges, but most of them were people I'd never heard of. I guessed they were probably really important people, but just not important in *interesting* ways.

Eventually Amanda and Cheryl finished yelling at each other and Amanda slammed the receiver down.

'At last!' I said, reaching for the phone.

'Excuse me,' Amanda said. 'What do you think you're doing?'

'I'm going to call Pippa,' I said.

'I haven't finished *my* calls yet,' Amanda said, picking up the phone and dialling another number. 'I have to speak to Rachel and Natalie. You can just wait your turn, Stacy.'

'I've been waiting for the past fifteen minutes,' I hollered.

'You're so impatient,' Amanda said. 'Don't you *ever* think of anyone but yourself?'

Can you *believe* that sister of mine? I felt like tying the phone cord around Amanda's ankles and hanging her upside down in the hallway as a warning to all self-centred, swollen-headed Bimbos not to push their younger sisters too far!

Amazing news! Apparently *Rachel* was through to the finals. And even more amazingly, super-vain aren't-I-gorgeous Natalie *wasn't*.

I finally got to speak to Pippa about forty minutes later. Uh-oh! Bad news. Pippa had gotten a letter from Blowbubble, but it didn't have an invitation card in it. It was a letter saying sorry but she'd been unsuccessful at the tryouts, better luck next time, and please accept a free one-dollar gift voucher to spend on a Blowbubble product of her choice.

The four of us met up at Fern's house that afternoon.

'I'm never going to buy Blowbubble Bubble Gum again!' Pippa said as she tore the free voucher into little tiny pieces in front of us. 'I wouldn't give them the satisfaction!'

'Way to be a good loser, Pippa,' Fern murmured.

'It's OK for you!' Pippa snapped. 'I don't get it! I just don't *get* it! How could they choose *you* and not me?'

Fern had gotten through to the finals.

'I guess Fern stood out,' Andy said to Pippa. 'And you didn't.' (That certainly was true!)

'It was those dumb glasses!' Pippa said.

'It was *not*,' Andy said.

'So, what was it?'

'I guess they were looking for something a little more, uh, eye-catching,' Andy said.

Pippa pointed at me. 'So how come Stacy got through? I'll tell you what this proves,' she said. 'It proves that they don't really want people who look like they have a *brain* in their head.'

I frowned at her. 'I'm going to try not to be totally *offended* by that,' I said. 'Just because I know you're upset.'

'Upset?' Pippa said. 'Who's upset? I'm not upset. Why should I be upset? For your information, I'm completely un-upset. In fact, I couldn't care less about the whole thing!' She went and sat huffily in a corner. 'I just don't want anything more to do with it, that's all!'

'OK,' Andy said, 'it's time to review the situation.'

'Huh?' Fern said.

'Two out of the three of us have gotten through to the finals,' Andy explained. 'Now we have to concentrate on making sure one of us wins.'

'What's with the *us*?' Fern said to Andy. 'I didn't notice you doing a whole lot. Oh, except loaning Pippa a pair of glasses she couldn't *see* through.'

'I'm going to ignore your lack of faith in me,' Andy said. 'And to show what a nice person I am, I'm still going to help both of you out.'

'Gee, thanks,' Fern said.

'OK,' Andy said. 'Let's take a look at the stuff they want you to do in the finals.'

According to the list, the tryout finals were going to be divided into three parts.

1. *'Bright-eyes and sunny smiles.' This is your chance to tell the panel of judges why you think you should be the Blowbubble Face of the Year. Points will be awarded for originality and appearance.*

2. *'The Real You.' Applicants will be asked questions about themselves. You can really shine, as you show the judges exactly what kind of special person you are. Points will be awarded for personality and presentation.*

3. *'Screen Test.' Applicants will be asked to perform in a make-believe television commercial for Blowbubble Bubble Gum. Points will be awarded for enthusiasm and photogenic qualities.*

'I have an idea for number two,' Andy said. 'We can hold pretend interviews. I'll be the interviewer.' He grabbed a hair brush from the dresser. 'This is the mike, OK?' he said. 'I'll interview Fern first.'

He shoved the hairbrush under Fern's nose.

'Would you like to tell us a little about your-self, Fern?' he said. 'Speak loudly and clearly, please.'

'MYNAMEISFERNKIPSAK!' Fern shout-ed into the hairbrush. 'AND I SHOULD BE THE BLOWBUBBLE FACE OF THE YEAR BECAUSE I CHEW LOADS OF BUBBLE GUM AND I LIKE IT AND BECAUSE I'M GONNA BEAT UP THE JUDGES IF I DON'T WIN!'

'Huh!' Pippa snorted from the corner. 'You can't say *that*. Even without the part about beating up the judges! You've got to say some-thing funny and unusual and cute, so they'll remember you.'

'I thought you didn't want anything more to do with this?' I said to Pippa.

'Yeah, well, I can't let you make total fools of yourselves,' Pippa said. 'Not if I can steer you in the right direction.'

Yeah, I thought to myself, that was all we needed. Andy *and* Pippa coaching us for the big day. Talk about the perfect way of making sure we came in last place!

'Now, for a start,' Pippa said to Fern, 'you need to learn to comb your hair properly.'

'Excuse me?' Fern said with an irritated glint in her eye.

Pippa blundered on. 'Face it, Fern. You

91

don't exactly look like you've just stepped out of a *salon.*'

'I like my hair this way,' Fern growled.

'You're joking, right?' Andy said. 'You mean you wear your hair like that on *purpose?*'

'That does it!' Fern said. 'I'm out of here!'

'Uh, Fern.' I said. This is *your* house.'

'Oh, yeah!' Fern said. 'So it is.' She pointed a commanding finger at Pippa. 'In that case, *you're* out of here.'

'Sorry?' Pippa said.

'And you!' Fern said to Andy. 'I have work to do. You two can go coach Stacy, if she's crazy enough to let you!'

The three of us stood on the pavement outside Fern's house.

'She'll never win with an attitude problem like that,' Pippa said. She looked at me. 'Anyhow,' she said with a big grin, 'this means we can devote all our attention to you, Stacy.'

'Uh, make a well-known phrase or saying out of the following words, guys,' I said, backing away. ' "Way" and "no".'

'But we want to help you!' Andy said.

'Thanks,' I said, hurrying along the street. 'I have to go right now. I have to, uh, feed my cat. I'll call you.'

I did call them, but only to tell them, as politely as I could, that I'd be just fine *without* a couple of crackpot coaches, and that I could rehearse perfectly well on my own.

But the next day I discovered that certain *other* people were rehearsing as well. And no way was I going to let my friends miss *that*!

* * *

'Shhh!' I hissed. 'Don't make a sound. If they hear you, they'll stop.'

Pippa, Fern and Andy and I were in our hall. I'd been watching through the living-room window for them to turn up, so I could let them in one by one without them ringing the bell. I didn't want Amanda and the Bimbos to know we were all in the house.

I'd called the gang about half an hour earlier and told them to get over here *right now* if they wanted to witness the funniest thing in the universe.

'Where are they?' Pippa whispered.

I pointed up the stairs and put my finger to my lips. We crept up the stairs, quiet as mice.

'Ow!' Andy said.

'Quiet!' I whispered. Huh, so much for *mice*! More like *elephants*!

'Fern stepped on my heel,' Andy complained.

'You should keep your big feet out of the way,' Fern said.

93

'Just shut up!' I whispered.

We crept up the rest of the stairs. Now we could hear the voices coming from Amanda's room.

A floorboard creaked under Pippa's foot and we all froze. Pippa mimed that it wasn't her fault. I made a mime back of strangling her and dumping her over the banister rail.

We tiptoed down the hall to Amanda's bedroom. A sheet of paper was taped to the door. It read, 'KEEP OUT. REHERSALS IN PROGRESS. DO NOT DISTURB.'

Pippa put her lips to my ear. 'That's not how you spell rehearsals,' she whispered.

I mimed to show that I couldn't care less how *rehearsals* was spelled, and furthermore, if she didn't keep quiet I'd nail her down under the carpet and run a steamroller over her. (It was quite a complicated mime, but I think Pippa got the general idea because she gave me an offended look and made the 'locked lips' sign to me.)

We spread out so there were two of us on either side of Amanda's door. We flattened ourselves against the wall and concentrated on listening.

And it was worth hearing!

'Well, Rachel,' we heard Natalie's squeaky voice saying, 'I'm sure everyone will have found your tips on how to deal with those tiresome split ends really, really fascinating and instructive. Now, I have a few more questions here which the judges would like to hear your views on.'

'I'd be more than happy to answer your questions, Natalie,' Rachel simpered. 'Please, fire away.'

'Uh, next question,' Natalie said. 'If you could change one thing in the world, Rachel, what would it be?'

'Well, there are so many things,' Rachel said. 'Uh, yeah, like, I can think of a *thousand* really bad things that I'd like to change. Like, uh, well, li–ike, um, ah . . .'

'Well, *name* one, Rachel,' Cheryl's cheese-grater voice chipped in. 'You sound like a total dork right now.'

'Cheryl, shut up!' Rachel said. 'You've made me forget what I was going to say. I had an idea then!'

'Huh!' Cheryl said. 'That would be a first.'

'Oh, right!' Rachel exclaimed. 'I'd like to see you do better.'

'No problem,' Cheryl said. 'OK, Natalie, interview *me* now. I'll show Rachel how to handle an interview.'

'No!' Rachel moaned. 'Natalie's interviewing me!'

There was the sound of a brief scuffle and then an 'Oww!' from Rachel and the thud of a backside hitting the floor.

'Careful, Rachel,' Amanda said. 'You'll break something.'

'Cheryl pushed me,' Rachel moaned.

'Stop whinging, Rachel,' Cheryl said. 'OK, Natalie, I'm ready.'

'Ooh! Ooh! I've thought of something!' Rachel squeaked. 'Ask me again, Natalie. I've got a real good answer!'

Natalie sounded like she was getting bored with being the interviewer. 'OK, Rachel, if you could change one thing in the world, what would it be?' she said flatly.

'Toenails!' Rachel said triumphantly.

Outside Amanda's room and back in the *real* world, Fern let out a splutter and had to cram both hands over her mouth to keep from laughing out loud.

'Toenails?' Cheryl shrieked. 'Are you out of your tiny mind?'

It was all I could do to bottle up the laughter that was threatening to explode out of me. I didn't dare look at the others or I really would have cracked up!

'I certainly am not!' Rachel exclaimed in a really dignified voice. 'Toenails are totally horrible, and if I could change one thing in the world, I'd get rid of toenails.'

'I know I'm gonna hate myself for asking this,' Amanda said. 'But why *toenails*, Rachel?'

'Isn't it obvious?' Rachel said. 'They get all that horrid *stuff* under them that you have to keep scraping out. And they grow, like, all the time, so you're always having to cut them. And if you don't cut them they just totally *bore* their way through your socks and stuff so you have to go buy new pairs when you could be spending the money on things that you really want. And big toenails get all *thick* and bent. They're like, totally disgusting.'

It all went quiet inside Amanda's bedroom.

'But toes would look really stupid without toenails,' Amanda said finally. 'They'd just be squishy little *blobs* on the end of your feet.'

'That's right,' Cheryl said, 'and if you want to get rid of toenails, Rachel, you'd have to get rid of fingernails, too. They're made out of the same stuff.'

'Ew!' Amanda squealed. 'Imagine fingers without fingernails! They'd be like some kind of *outer space* things. Like *tentacles* or something. Ew, Rachel, that's *horrible*!'

'I never mentioned fingernails,' Rachel said. 'I don't want to get rid of fingernails. That's just stupid!'

'This is totally ridiculous!' Natalie squealed at the top of her voice. 'You guys are nuts! What are you talking about, toenails? That's not what the question means at all!'

'So what does it mean, smartypants?' Rachel asked.

'You're supposed to come up with something like world peace or the brotherhood of man or an end to pollution or stuff like that,' Natalie squeaked. 'They won't want to hear a load of junk about *toenails*!'

'How do you know what the question means?' Cheryl said.

'Because I made it up!' Natalie said. 'So I know what it means, OK? Rachel made up the question on tips for looking good. Amanda made up the question about a favourite vacation destination. You made up the one about the formula for the perfect party, and I made up the one about changing one thing in the world.'

'Well, yeah, OK,' Cheryl admitted. 'But it was a dumb question, anyway.'

'Was not!'

'Was, too!'

'Uh, guys,' Amanda said. 'Maybe we should quit it with the interview part, huh? We can come back to it later.'

'I don't care what we do,' Natalie said.

'Seeing how I'm not even *in* the finals for some reason that makes no sense whatsoever. And I'd just like to say *again* that whoever made the choices had to be insane to let a total freak like *Stacy* through, but dropped me!'

Freak! What a nerve!

'Look, I didn't make it to the finals either,' Cheryl said, 'but you don't hear me complaining.'

'You were complaining on the phone to me for half an hour about it last night,' Rachel said.

'Oh, shut up, Rachel,' Cheryl said. 'Amanda? What was the next thing on that list?'

'Well,' Amanda said, 'there's the screen test part, or we could go over the 'Bright-eyes, sunny smiles' part again. My gran showed me this really neat way of learning how to walk properly.'

'What's to learn?' Rachel said. 'I already know how to walk properly.'

'Yeah,' Fern whispered, 'with your *knuckles* scraping the ground!'

We all spluttered with laughter at this.

'Did you guys hear something?' Natalie said.

I almost crammed my fist into my mouth to keep quiet. I tried to give Fern a glare but she was too busy clutching her ribs and chewing her lips to keep from screaming. Andy had slid down to the carpet and had his face jammed against his knees. His shoulders were bouncing up and down. Pippa had both hands over her face and looked like she was crying with laughter.

'I don't hear anything,' Cheryl said. 'So, Amanda? What's this way of learning to walk properly?'

'You use a book,' Amanda explained. 'It teaches you to walk really smoothly and totally upright and, like, completely elegantly. Like catwalk models do, you know?'

'Sounds OK,' Cheryl said. 'I'll give it a try. Got a *book*, Amanda?'

'Yeah, here's one,' Amanda said.

Amanda had *books* in her room? Oh, yeah, I remembered! She had some great big art books. She must have given Cheryl one of those.

'It's kind of heavy,' Cheryl said. 'I don't want to end up with bowed legs. So? What do I do?'

Right then, I really wished I could see what was going on in there. I'd have loved to see Cheryl drop a heavy book on her foot!

'Keep your head up,' Amanda instructed her. 'If you're doing it right, the book shouldn't even move. Now, walk over to the window. No, don't look down. Keep looking straight ahead. Yeah. That's fine. Now walk back across the room.'

'Ow!' Natalie squealed. 'That's my foot, you clumsy idiot!'

'Sorry,' Cheryl said. 'I can't see what's going on down there, I— oops!' There was a dull thud.

'*Yee-oww*!' Natalie wailed. 'My *head*!'

'Sorry!'

'I don't see why Cheryl should be trying it out, anyhow,' Rachel said. 'Only Amanda and I are in the finals. You two should be helping us prepare. Come on, give me that book, Cheryl. I wanna try it out.'

'You want me to give you the book, huh?' Cheryl said.

'Yes, I certainly do.'

'There you go!' *Clump*!

'Owww! That hurt!'

'Quit messing around, guys,' Amanda said. 'I don't want that book damaged.'

'Cheryl hit me on purpose!' Rachel moaned.

'I don't know what you're complaining about,' Cheryl said. 'Your skull is thicker than a whale sandwich! Just balance it on your head, Rachel, and make like a fashion model.'

There was quiet in there for a few moments.

'Hey, not bad!' Amanda said. 'It didn't even wobble!'

'It's because I flattened her head a little when I hit her,' Cheryl said.

'Like I said,' Rachel said smugly. 'I already *know* how to walk.'

'My gran said a person should be able to walk up an entire flight of stairs without the book falling off,' Amanda said.

'OK,' Rachel said. 'Open the door for me and I'll go walk up and down the stairs a couple of times.'

Uh-oh! Time to get out of there. Except that we *didn't* have time to get out of there. The door opened about two seconds later and Rachel came sailing out into the hall, balancing a really big hardback book on her head.

And the first thing that happened as she turned towards the top of the stairs was that she tripped over Pippa's foot.

'Ow!' Pippa howled.

'What the—' Rachel nearly jumped out of her skin in surprise. The book teetered, slid and dropped. '*Yee-owwwch!*' Rachel shrieked as the book whacked down edgewise right on *her* foot.

Fern and Andy just *yelled* with laughter as

Rachel started hopping around the hall, clutching her foot in both hands.

'What the heck is going on out here?' Amanda hollered. Then she saw the four of us lined up against the wall. 'YOU!'

'Run!' I yelled to the others as Amanda's hand grabbed for me. If we could get into my room in the next three seconds and bar the door somehow, then we might be safe. If not, I reckoned we'd probably all be killed right there in Amanda's bedroom doorway.

Chapter Eleven

We weren't killed. Luckily Mom came up to check out all the thumping and yelling and so we escaped the dreaded Vengeance of the Killer Bimbos. Well, maybe *luckily* isn't quite the right word.

Have you heard the expression: *out of the frying pan into the fire*? It means something like: saved from the Killer Bimbos only to be yelled at by Bad-mood Mom.

Mom was in a *really* bad mood. It was worse than a yelling mood. It was one of her rare volcano-about-to-explode moods. She sent all my friends and all the Bimbos home and grounded Amanda and me for the rest of the day.

'But, Mom,' Amanda pleaded, 'I have to practise for the finals on Saturday. How can I practise if I can't see my friends?'

'Practise in front of Stacy,' Mom growled. 'But do it *quietly*. If I hear one more sound out of you two I'll ground you for a *week*.'

'Aw, Mom,' Amanda said with one of her sweet little smiles, 'then I'd miss the finals.'

Mom gave her a hard look. 'Do you really think I care two figs about that stupid bubble gum contest, Amanda? Trust me, I've got other things to think about right now.'

Something a smart person needs to know about my Mom is that there are times when *arguing* with her is a really bad idea. Like, right *then*, for instance, was a very bad time.

'I think maybe you should go to your room, Amanda,' Mom said. 'Before I get really annoyed with you.'

'What?' Amanda just stood there as if she couldn't believe her ears.

'Go!' Mom yelled.

Amanda went. I went, too.

Mom headed back down to her basement office.

'Phew!' Amanda breathed as she walked into her room. 'What a grouch! A person can't even *breathe* around here.'

'You are so *dumb* sometimes,' I told her. 'Couldn't you tell she was already in a really bad mood?'

Amanda frowned at me, fists on her hips. 'And you go upsetting her even more, Stacy! And nearly getting both of us grounded for an entire week. That's just typical of you! Totally thoughtless.'

'Wha-a-a-at?'

Amanda wagged a finger in my face. 'If you and your idiot friends hadn't been creeping around out here and making fun of us, none of this would have happened. It's all *your* fault, Stacy, and there's no point in you denying it.'

'You're right,' I said.

'Don't you try to weasel out of it, Stacy.'

'I said you're *right*!' I said. 'I was agreeing with you.'

'Oh.' Amanda looked like the wind had been taken right out of her sails. 'Well,' she said, 'Fine. I should think so, too!'

'The thing is,' I said. 'How do we find out what's bugging Mom?'

'I bet the bad mood is just because she has so much work to do,' Amanda said. 'Dad said she was being asked to do heaps of work right now.' Amanda tossed her hair. 'Being asked to do too much work would get anyone down.'

I couldn't help laughing. 'How would you know?'

'I do plenty of work, for your information,' Amanda said. 'That cheerleading squad doesn't just run itself, you know. And the clothes I wear don't just fall into my arms out of the sky. I have to really search the mall for the best stuff. And do you think my hair gets like this all on its own, Stacy?'

'Yeah, OK,' I said. 'I get the picture. You're a total *slave*, Amanda. But what are we going to do to help cheer Mom up?'

'We'll be extra-special super-nice to her,' Amanda said. 'And we can start by taking her a really thoughtful snack. A cup of coffee and a blueberry muffin.'

'Good idea,' I said. 'And maybe we could do some housework for her?'

Amanda looked at me. 'Let's not go crazy here, Stacy. Let's just fetch her the snack and tell her we promise to be totally quiet and helpful. And I don't mean *doing chores* kind of helpful. I mean staying-out-of-the-way kind of helpful, right?'

'Right.'

I don't know if it was the cup of coffee or the blueberry muffin or what, but Mom apologized for yelling at us. She even switched her computer off right in the middle of some work and sat and talked with us for a while, which is something she'd never usually do.

'Is there something wrong?' I asked her. 'Is your work getting you down?'

Mom smiled. 'It doesn't help,' she said. 'But, no, that's not the problem.'

'Is there something else?' Amanda said. 'You can tell us.'

'Yes, OK,' Mom said. 'I guess we shouldn't keep things from you, and it'll probably all come to nothing.' She took a deep breath. 'There are some changes happening in the firm where your father works.'

'Oh!' Of course! That letter Dad had received from work!

'Has he been fired?' Amanda breathed.

'No, nothing as bad as that,' Mom said. 'But the firm has been taken over by another company and there are a lot of rumours flying around up there. When companies get taken over, the new bosses usually start off by changing everything to suit themselves. And right now your dad doesn't know what's going to happen to him. And when your dad is worried, I get worried, too.'

'They won't fire him,' I said confidently. 'Dad's a totally brilliant salesman. Hey, they might even promote him.'

'Yes, why not?' Mom said with a grin. 'He deserves it, with all that travelling he does.'

'And if he gets promoted,' Amanda said, 'maybe he won't have to spend so much time on the road.'

'Let's keep our fingers crossed, huh, girls?' Mom said. 'But whatever happens, it was wrong of me to take my bad mood out on you.'

Well, that sure cleared the air.

Amanda and I had agreed not to mention the Blowbubble finals on Saturday.

So, after we'd finished talking about Dad, we talked about a bunch of other things. After a while Mom said she'd better get back to work or she'd have the publisher on her case *again*. We were just on our way back upstairs – Mission Cheer Up Mom accomplished, when Amanda turned back.

'I don't want to make a big thing out of this,' she said, 'but are you and Dad coming to the finals on Saturday?' She gave Mom a big smile. 'I thought you *might*, as both your daughters are going to be there and one of them stands a pretty good chance of winning, in my opinion.'

No prizes for guessing which one of us Amanda thought had a good chance of winning.

'Your father will be in Chicago,' Mom said.

'He will?' I said in surprise. 'But Dad told me he wouldn't be working weekends for a while.'

'It's something to do with the take-over,' Mom said. 'The company has called a special meeting and everyone has to be there. Believe me, he'd much rather be down here with us, but he doesn't have the choice.'

Amanda sighed deeply and carried on walking up the stairs. 'Well,' she called back, 'when I'm a millionaire movie star with my own private psychoanalyst, I'll just have to tell him that all my deep psychological wounds were caused by my father being forced to go to some dumb meeting in Chicago and missing my totally amazing debut!'

Mom didn't say anything. She just turned back to her computer and started typing. That wasn't like Mom at all.

★   ★   ★

But Mom wasn't the only person acting funny that day. I discovered Amanda doing something that Amanda *never* does.

I went down to the kitchen later that afternoon and I found Amanda in there with an apron on, reading a recipe from a magazine. She was standing over the chopping board and hacking away at some avocados with a big knife. This may not *sound* like much, but believe me, I catch Amanda working in the kitchen about as often as I catch my cat, Benjamin, reciting poetry.

She even had the food processor all connected.

'What are you doing?' I asked. 'If you're fixing dinner, I'm eating out.'

'I'm preparing a *facial*,' Amanda said as she scraped chopped up pieces of avocado into the food processor.

'You're doing *what*?'

She turned the food processor on.

'It's the natural way to refresh tired skin, reduce fine dryness lines and renew your skin's natural elasticity,' Amanda howled above the roar of the motor. She prodded the magazine. 'It says so in here.'

It did, too. And it had pictures of girls with green slime all over their faces and slices of cucumber on their eyes.

Amanda switched off and scraped the green goo into a bowl.

'Do you think Mom would let me try this grape diet?' she asked, pointing to another part of the page. 'See? For three days you don't eat anything but grapes. Literally *all* the top models do it.'

'Why?' I asked.

'To cleanse and purify their bodies,' Amanda said. 'It stops you getting zits and stuff like that.'

'But why grapes?'

'Beats me,' Amanda said. 'Do I look like a nutritional scientist?'

'With that avocado stuff all over your face you'll look more like some kind of swamp monster,' I said.

'For your information,' Amanda said. 'An avocado facial can increase your skin's natural radiance by up to seventy-three per cent.'

I stared at her. 'What the heck does that mean?'

'Uh, it means that . . . well, the thing is,' Amanda consulted the magazine. 'It's, like, a scientifically worked-out formula,' she said. 'You wouldn't understand it.' She tapped the magazine. 'But it says so in here, so it must be true.'

She picked up her bowl of avocado facial goo. 'Tell everyone not to disturb me for an hour,' she said. She opened the fridge, pulled a cucumber out of the salad tray and tucked it under her arm.

'What do you mean, *everyone*?' I asked. 'Who are you expecting to drop by, Amanda? A couple of movie directors? A fashion photographer? Thelonius Appleby?'

'I'll be in my room,' Amanda said, ignoring me. 'Making myself even more beautiful than usual.'

She marched upstairs. Benjamin came prowling in through the cat flap and rubbed against my legs.

'Our big sister is completely crazy, Benjamin,' I told him.

'*Browwwlll*,' Benjamin said, which usually means, *Feed me now.*

I was just forking some food into Benjamin's bowl when Mom came up from the basement.

'Finished!' she said, wiping her arm across her forehead. 'That should keep them happy for a while.' She walked over to the counter. 'Hey, who's been cooking?'

'Amanda,' I said.

Mom peered into the food processor. 'She's made the guacamole already,' she said, looking really pleased.

'She's made *what*?'

Mom smiled. 'Once in a while your sister can be really helpful,' she said. 'I bought some avocados so I could make *guacamole*. It's Mexican and you eat it with tortilla chips. I was just going to make it, but it looks like Amanda beat me to it.'

'I see,' I said slowly. 'A special treat, huh?'

'I'm really looking forward to it,' Mom said. 'Did she put it in the fridge? You're supposed to chill it for a little while.'

'No,' I said, sidling towards the door. 'She didn't *exactly* put it in the fridge.'

Mom looked around. 'So where did she put it, honey?' she asked. 'Honey? Hey! Stacy!'

But I was out of there! If anyone was going to explain where Amanda had put the guacamole, it sure wasn't going to be me.

Chapter Twelve

'I still think you could have made something up,' Amanda said to me. 'Like, you could have told Mom that dumb cat of yours ate the yucky-moley stuff.'

'*Guacamole*,' I corrected her for the millionth time. 'I don't see why Benjamin should have gotten into trouble on your behalf.'

We were in the mall. Amanda was still mad at me. She thought I should have helped her out over the avocado incident. But like I'd been telling her over and over, what was I supposed to do?

'Anyway,' I said, 'you're lucky Mom saw the funny side of it. She could have grounded you for a *month*.' Mom had grounded Amanda for an additional day. Which I thought was pretty laid-back for a person who had just seen her special dip smeared all over her daughter's face.

'She might as well have done!' Amanda moaned. 'There's only one more day to the finals, and I've hardly had a *chance* to rehearse with the guys. And the first day Mom lets me out of the house at all, I have to go to the supermarket to pick up some more of those dumb avocados. *And* I have to pay for them. I ask you, is that fair?'

'Quit moaning,' I said. 'I thought you said you were going to *walk* the finals.'

'I am,' Amanda said uncertainly. 'Of course I am.'

'But?' I asked.

Amanda looked at me. 'Why was Judy so totally confident that she was going to win when we met her at the ice rink the other day?'

'Beats me,' I said. 'Maybe she's planning on bribing the judges.'

Amanda stared at me. 'You think so?'

'No, of course not,' I said. 'She's just got a swollen head. You know what she's like. She thinks she's best at everything.'

'Yeah, I guess so,' Amanda said. 'It's a real pity she can't do something useful, like have an accident the day before.'

'You shouldn't wish things like that on people,' I warned her. 'Bad wishes can come back to you!'

'I only meant a teeny-weenie accident,' Amanda said. 'I don't want her *dead*,

116

especially. I'd just like her *not* to be able to make the finals, that's all.'

I gave Amanda a long, thoughtful look. 'Are you worried that she might win?' I asked.

'No! No way! Huh! As if!' Amanda protested. 'But . . . well, the judges might make the *wrong* decision. They might have really bizarre ideas about who looks good. I mean, what if the judges don't like blonde hair? What if they're all really into girls with *black* hair?'

'It isn't only about good looks,' I reminded her. 'It's about personality, too.'

'Judy can really turn on the charm when she wants to,' Amanda said.

'So can you,' I said.

'But what if she does it better on the day?'

'Then I guess you'll lose, and you'll have to quit the cheerleading squad,' I said.

'Don't say that!' Amanda wailed. 'I knew it! You think I'm going to lose!'

'I do *not*!' I said. 'I think you're going totally crazy. I mean, what makes you so sure *either* of you will win?' I tried to do an Amanda-type toss with my hair. It didn't really work. 'After all,' I said, 'there are *other* people in these finals.'

'What? Rachel, you mean?' Amanda said. 'She won't win!'

'No, not Rachel. Me.'

'Oh, *you*!' Amanda snorted.

'Excuse me!'

'I'm sorry,' Amanda said, patting me annoyingly on the head. 'Of course you have a really good chance of winning, Stacy. But it's not you that I've made the bet with. It's that prize-winning sleaze-bag, Judy.'

'Uh-oh, talk of the devil,' I said. I nudged Amanda and pointed over to a really high-class clothes shop. Judy MacWilliams and her semi-human sidekick, Maddie Fischer, were just walking out. Judy was carrying a bag. New clothes for the finals, I guessed.

'Oh, great,' Amanda moaned. 'Judy and the Toad, in *person*. This makes my day absolutely *perfect*!'

Judy spotted us straight away and made a point of strutting over with Maddie blobbing along behind her.

'Well, *hello-o*,' Judy chirped. 'If it isn't the two losers.' She smirked at Amanda. 'I hope you've made plans for all the free time you're gonna have after you quit the cheerleaders, Amanda.'

'I'm not going to have to quit,' Amanda said. 'And I hope *you've* started writing your speech to the school about what a big, stupid, brain-dead idiot you are.'

'I don't think that'll be necessary,' Judy said.

'You know, Amanda, I've been thinking. When I take over the cheerleading squad, I might change the uniforms a little. I was thinking of having your *face* printed on the back of the skirts so everyone can show exactly what they think of you every time they sit down.'

Maddie made a snorkelling, bubbling noise; it was her way of laughing. It sounded like an octopus sucking sludge up through a drainpipe. (It did; trust me!)

Amanda took a step towards Judy so that the two of them were nose-to-nose.

Judy looked a little uneasy, like she was worried that Amanda was going to punch her lights out.

'You have little broken veins in the whites of your eyes, Judy,' Amanda said coolly. 'You should do something about them before your eyes go completely *pink*.'

'I'll see you Saturday, *loser*,' Judy hissed. Then she turned and marched off. Maddie went scuttling after her. The two of them got onto the escalator and sank out of sight.

'I hope you beat Judy,' I said.

'Why, *thank you*, Stacy,' Amanda said in surprise. 'That's a really nice thing to say.' She put her arm around my shoulders.

'Uh, hold up,' I said. 'I don't mean I hope

you *win*. *I'm* gonna win. I just hope you beat *Judy*.'

Amanda took her arm away and gave me an expressive look.

'She's really confident,' I said. 'Maybe she has plans to sabotage you.'

'Like how?'

'Well,' I said, 'remember that *Cheerleader Champions* movie, where the girl had red paint tipped all over her just before she was due to go on stage at the talent contest?'

'That was a *movie*, Stacy,' Amanda said. 'People don't do things like that in real life. Not even *Judy*.'

'I guess you're right,' I said. 'But if I were you, I'd be keeping my eyes open on Saturday. Judy is definitely up to something.'

★ ★ ★

Dad wasn't home in time for dinner that night. Not that there was anything unusual in that; when a person has to drive all the way up to Chicago to get to his head office, then a person is going to miss dinner at home *plenty* of times.

Sometimes Dad had to stay away for two or three days in a row and sleep in motels and eat lonely motel breakfasts and miserable stuff like that. I guess I'd kind of gotten used to

Dad being away so much, but I still didn't *like* it at all.

Maybe all the changes that were happening in his company might mean that Dad would be home more. That would be totally brilliant. I was going to keep my fingers crossed and hope that his new bosses would decide to open an office right here in Four Corners.

While we were eating Amanda was still grumbling about Dad not being able to get to the Blowbubble finals.

'OK,' Mom said finally, '*I'll* come.'

'But you don't approve of it,' Amanda said. 'I thought you hated the whole thing.'

'Look,' Mom said, putting her knife and fork down. 'I'll admit I wasn't happy about the pair of you getting too obsessive about this competition.' She sighed. 'But if you're determined to do it, then I figure I should be right there to cheer you on.' She smiled at us. 'Now, quit grouching, Amanda. If either of you wins tomorrow, I'll be there to see it, and I'll be cheering from the rafters, OK?'

Way to go, Mom!

Amanda gobbled her food.

'I have to call Cheryl,' she said. 'We need to get some last-minute rehearsals in!'

'Me, too,' I said as both of us ran for the phone. 'I need to call Pippa!'

We wrestled for the receiver.

'Guys,' Mom called from the kitchen, 'I said I didn't want you getting too *obsessive* about this thing!'

We fought like crazy to get the phone out of each other's hands.

Obsessive? Who was getting obsessive?

In the end I figured out that Mom must have meant Amanda. I mean, who else would wind up sitting on a person's *head* in order to make a phone call?

Chapter Thirteen

The Big Day started really, really badly for
Amanda. She got the worst phone call of her
life!

Well, actually the day *started* with Amanda
locking herself in the bathroom with her CD
player and about a gallon of bubble bath, and
soaking in there for over an hour.

I was beginning to think she must have
turned into some kind of mermaid-sister-thing
by the time she finally came wandering out in
her robe. She was bright pink from all the
steam.

'At last!' I said. 'Can I finally get in there
now, or do you want to *hog* the bathroom for
another couple of hours?'

'It's all yours,' Amanda said airily. Sarcasm
is wasted on Amanda.

She seemed a whole lot less jittery about
the finals now. In fact, from the way she
elbowed me aside in the hall and strolled into
her room, you'd think she'd already won.

Then it happened!

The phone rang.

'I'll get it,' Amanda called, running down the stairs. 'It's probably Rachel hyperventilating or something.'

I went into the bathroom.

A few minutes later I came out and leaned over the banisters. Amanda was sitting on the stairs with the hung up phone in her lap. She was just *staring* into space with her face as white as a sheet.

'What's wrong?' I called down cheerfully. 'Has Rachel's hair all fallen out?'

Amanda stared up at me. I got a really queasy feeling in my stomach. Amanda looked *terrible*.

'That was the bubble gum people,' she said blankly. 'There's been a mistake. I got the wrong letter. They said it was some kind of administrative error. They said they were really sorry.'

I ran down the stairs. Amanda's eyes were brimming with tears.

'I-I'm not in the finals at all,' she gulped. 'I want Mom!'

I ran and fetched Mom from the kitchen. Amanda just clung onto her with tears running down her face.

Amanda was in such a bad way that I almost burst out crying myself.

After a few minutes, Mom managed to calm Amanda down enough for Amanda to tell her exactly what had happened.

'It was some woman,' Amanda hiccoughed, wiping her face on the sleeves of her robe. 'From the Chicago office. She said they sent me the wrong letter by mistake and that I wasn't in the finals at all.'

Mom gave her a big hug. 'Oh, sweetheart, I'm so sorry,' Mom said. 'How could they *do* that to someone! That is just so *unreasonable*!'

'It was a mistake,' Amanda mumbled into Mom's shoulder.

'Mistake!' Mom growled. 'I'll give them *mistake*! Do you have their phone number?'

'Sure,' Amanda said. 'Why?'

'Because I'm going to call them and give them a piece of my mind,' Mom said. 'I won't have you let down like this! What do they think they're up to?'

I ran and got one of the Blowbubble Bubble Gum letters for Mom. I sure didn't envy those guys on the other end of the phone. My mom was going to tear them to little pieces!

Except that no one at the Chicago office knew anything about the phone call to Amanda.

Mom was given another number to call. Ed Munrow's mobile phone number.

'There's something screwy going on here,' Mom said as she dialled the new number. 'Are you sure the woman you spoke to said she was in Chicago?'

Amanda nodded.

Mom wasn't the only one getting kind of suspicious.

'What did the woman sound like?' I asked Amanda.

'I don't know,' Amanda said. 'Kind of *nasal*. Youngish, I guess. It was just some *woman*.'

'Are you sure it wasn't just some *girl* holding her nose and speaking real low?' I asked.

'Huh?'

'Oh, hello,' Mom said into the phone. 'Could I speak to Ed Munrow, please?' Pause. 'Yes! It is urgent! I want to speak to him right *now*!'

Amanda and I listened while Mom spoke to Ed Munrow.

Through the call she went from being really angry, to sounding confused and then ending up totally apologetic.

She put the phone down and looked at us.

'Mr Munrow said he doesn't know anything about a phone call,' she said. She looked at

Amanda. 'He said you're definitely on the finals list.'

'It was a prank call,' Amanda gasped.

Amanda and I looked at each other.

'It was *her*!' Amanda yelled. 'I should have guessed!'

'If this is your friend Cheryl's idea of a joke—' Mom began.

'Not Cheryl, Mom,' Amanda gabbled. 'Judy rat-fink MacWilliams!'

It took us a little while to fill Mom in on the way Judy had been acting recently. So this was the ace up her sleeve! She obviously had the fake call planned right from the start! No wonder she was so sure Amanda wasn't going to win. She had it all set up so that Amanda wouldn't even *be* there.

'I'm calling her parents right now,' Mom said angrily. 'I think they should know what a nasty piece of work their daughter is.'

'No, Mom, don't,' Amanda said. 'It's OK, really it is.'

'It is not, Amanda!' Mom said. 'You were crying your eyes out five minutes ago.'

'I'm fine now,' Amanda said. 'Really I am. Please, Mom, let me deal with Judy.'

Mom relented. 'Well, OK,' she said, 'but you just make sure you tell her exactly what I think of her.'

'Oh, don't worry,' Amanda said grimly. 'I'll do that, OK. She's not getting away with this. No way!'

★ ★ ★

I can't *tell* you what our house was like from then on that morning. Try imagining a typhoon and a whirlwind meeting together in a place where a volcano is erupting while an earthquake takes place.

Now add a really colossal thunderstorm and a tidal wave.

Then imagine all of that packed into the shape of my sister Amanda, hurtling around the place like a hyperactive pinball.

She tried on *eight* different outfits. In the end I just sat to one side on the stairs and watched her go streaking up and down past me. First she'd hurtle down to the basement to ask Mom's opinion. Then she asked my opinion. Then she said I didn't know what I was talking about. *Then* she called Cheryl, Natalie and Rachel on the phone. First of all she told them all about Judy's nasty, rotten, underhand trick, and then she described what she was wearing at that moment, and asked *their* opinions. And then she raced back to her room to try something completely different.

I don't know why she had to make such a

total drama out of getting dressed! I mean, I managed to choose my outfit without all that racing about. I was wearing a short-sleeved blue top and a blue skirt. Mom said I looked really, really nice. OK, so it wasn't totally *glamorous*, but then I wasn't going for the glamorous look.

It was getting late. I'd been ready for *ages*, but Amanda was still undecided when James arrived. He'd agreed to go with us to the sports centre. For moral support, Amanda said. To stop her going completely insane, I thought. Except that he was too late for that. My sister had been completely insane for the past five hours.

Amanda told James about Judy's call. He said he wasn't the least little bit surprised. He said he thought Judy was capable of just about *anything*. He also said he was sure Amanda would beat her, which was exactly what Amanda wanted to hear.

At *last* Amanda hit on an outfit that she liked. A yellow dress and a really nice blue jacket. She had a yellow band in her hair and a gold necklace.

She stood at the top of the stairs.

'Well?' she said.

'Perfect,' Mom said from down in the hallway. 'You look like an angel. You'll knock 'em dead, honey.'

'Totally excellent,' I said, glancing at my watch. 'Can we please *go*, now?' There was only half an hour before we needed to be at the sports centre. The last thing I wanted was for Amanda to rip the outfit off and start all over!

'James?' Amanda asked. 'Is it OK?'

'It's great,' James said. 'Honest!'

'Sure?' Amanda asked anxiously. 'I could try a different coloured top.'

'No!' we all yelled.

We almost had to *drag* Amanda to the car.

'Maybe red would be better than yellow,' she said as we crammed her into the back. 'Or maybe I should wear a skirt and top.'

I sat in the front and held Sam on my lap as Mom drove down the road. Mom was going to drop us off, then take Sam over to Gran and Grandad's, and then get back to the sports centre in time to watch the finals.

I looked around at Amanda. She was sitting bolt-upright, staring straight ahead with a fixed manic grin on her face.

'Stop the car!' Amanda howled suddenly, yanking at the door handle. 'I *hate* this outfit. I look like a nerd!'

'James,' Mom ordered, 'hold her down!

Listen, Amanda, no way are we turning around, OK? You look just fine the way you are.'

'I don't!' Amanda wailed. 'I look ridiculous!'

Somehow James managed to keep Amanda from escaping out of the car until we arrived at the sports centre. There were plenty of people around, and a whole lot of parked cars.

'I'll drive up to the front entrance,' Mom said. 'But there's nowhere to park. So you'll just have to jump out, OK?'

'Are you back to normal now?' I asked Amanda.

'I'm fine,' Amanda gabbled. 'Absolutely fine. Just fine, OK? I'm completely and totally *fine*! Everything is completely and utterly FINE! Why are you all *staring* at me like that? I tell you I'm perfectly *FINE*! What is it with you people?'

Mom chuckled to herself. 'Good luck, both of you,' she said. She winked at James. 'Look after them, James.'

'You don't need to look after me,' I said in a dignified way as I got out of the car and strapped Sam's baby seat in place. '*I'm* OK.'

'And, hey!' Mom called to Amanda. 'Don't you get into an argument with Judy, you hear?'

'Sure thing, Mom,' Amanda said, a little too easily, if you asked me.

'Just tell her calmly and quietly,' Mom continued, 'that practical jokes like that phone call this morning aren't *funny* at all.'

'Got it, Mom,' Amanda said. 'Calmly and quietly. OK.'

Mom gave her an uneasy look. There are times with Amanda when the things she says just don't seem to match up with the expression on her face, if you know what I mean.

Amanda *sounded* cool, but to my mind, she looked kind of *homicidal* whenever Judy's name was mentioned.

Once Sam was safely tucked into his seat, Mom waved and drove off. Amanda closed her eyes and took several long, deep breaths.

'OK,' she said in a completely calm voice. 'Let's go get famous!'

Chapter Fourteen

'Know what I think would be a really good idea when we see Judy?' I said as we made our way into the crowded foyer. 'I think it would be a really good idea if we, like, totally *ignored* her!'

'Cute plan, Stacy,' Amanda said dryly, 'I can see how that would teach her a lesson she'd never forget.'

The whole of the foyer was full of Blowbubble merchandise again, as well as posters and banners and loudspeakers playing carousel music.

'So, what are you going to do?' James asked. 'Should I have a paramedic team on standby?'

'James, *please*,' Amanda said. 'Do I look like some kind of total axe-wielding maniac? You heard what Mom said. I'm going to be completely calm and utterly quiet. I'm just going to take her to one side and tell her a few home truths. And then I'm going to concentrate on winning this competition.'

A voice sounded over the loudspeaker:

'Will all finalists please make their way to level two and through the blue doors to your left,' the voice announced. 'All finalists have to be registered. If you do not register you will not be allowed to compete, so hurry along through the *blue* doors, please. Non-finalists should make their way through the *red* doors over to your right and into the main hall.'

I looked around for my friends, but there was no sign of any of them. Either they hadn't arrived yet, or they'd already gone through.

'I'll see you later, then,' James said. 'Good luck.'

'Luck won't come into it,' Amanda said coolly. 'I am just too perfect to lose, and that's all there is to it!'

I looked at her. It was hard to believe that not five minutes ago she'd been a gibbering wreck in the back of our car!

James made his way towards the red doors and Amanda and I joined the trickle of people heading up the stairs. I noticed that there were nearly as many boys as there were girls. There seemed to be people all the way from about seven or eight right up to teenagers of fourteen or fifteen. Some of them were kind of good-looking, but quite a few of them didn't look any more glamorous than *me*. One thing was for sure, this certainly wasn't a *beauty* contest.

We went through the doors and joined a line of people in the hallway. And that was when it happened. Despite everything that Amanda had said, that was when World War *Three* broke out.

I was still looking around for Fern, so I hardly noticed Judy. But Amanda noticed her! Boy, did Amanda notice her!

The first I knew of it was when Amanda's fingers closed around my arm and she seemed to be trying to pull it off. And there was a hissing noise coming from her, like escaping steam.

'Sh-sh-sh-she,' Amanda hissed. 'Sh-sh-she's there.'

I looked along the line. Judy was about nine people ahead, with her back turned to us.

Right at the front of the line was a big tangle of carrot-red hair and a skinny body in a lime green dress. It was Rachel. She was looking back over the line, stretching her long, skinny neck like a giraffe in a fright-wig.

She caught sight of Amanda and called out.

'Hey! Amanda! Hi! It's me!' (As if anyone else would wear *that* shade of green!)

Of course, Judy looked around, too. And that was when Judy saw Amanda. And Judy's eyes went kind of *circular*, like she'd just seen a ghost. And her face went white and her mouth fell open.

Amanda stepped out of line and walked slowly along to where Judy was standing.

'Hi, Judy,' she said. 'Catching flies? With a mouth *that* size I guess you could catch *buzzards*!'

Judy closed her mouth.

'You look surprised to see me,' Amanda said smoothly. 'Did you think maybe I wasn't going to turn up?'

'I don't know what you're talking about,' Judy said. She gave a little toss of her long black hair and turned away from Amanda like she'd *finished* with her.

'I think you do!' Amanda snapped, grabbing Judy's shoulder and jerking her back so they were face to face again.

'Hey, get your hands off me,' Judy snarled. 'I should call the organizers and have you thrown out.'

'You just try it, Judy,' Amanda said. 'I'm sure they'd like to hear how you faked that call this morning so that I'd think I wasn't in the finals.'

Judy looked around at the other people in the line. The two of them certainly were the centre of attention. Judy tapped the side of her head and smirked.

'She's spent too much time in the sun,' she said. 'It's fried her brain.'

'You're so funny, Judy,' Amanda said. 'Let's see how funny you are when you try explaining to the judges why you made that call to my house this morning.'

A huge grin stretched clear across Judy's face.

'Let me get this clear,' Judy said slowly. 'You want me to go see the competition judges?'

'Got it in one.'

'That's fine with me,' Judy said. 'Only let's go right to the top, huh? I think we should go see the chairman of the judges' panel. I think maybe you should tell your little story to him.' She gave Amanda a big smile. 'Does that sound OK to you, Amanda?'

Uh-oh, I was thinking. *Judy's up to something.* I couldn't figure *what*, but she sure had something up her sleeve!

'That sounds fine,' Amanda said.

Call me super-suspicious, but I had the feeling that Judy was leading Amanda right into some kind of horrible *trap*.

That was when Rachel decided to help out. She stepped out of line and marched up to Judy and Amanda.

'Hey, what's the problem?' she said to Amanda. 'Need any help?'

'Hey, who left your cage open?' Judy said. 'Get lost, gibbon-girl!'

'It's OK,' Amanda said to Rachel. 'I can handle it.'

But it was too late.

'What did you call me?' Rachel growled at Judy.

'Deaf as well as dumb, huh?' Judy said.

Rachel made as if to grab Judy. Judy ducked back just as Amanda lurched forwards to stop Rachel.

Amanda bumped into Judy. Somehow Rachel tripped backwards over her big feet and ended up on her rear end on the floor. Judy gave Amanda a shove. Amanda turned and shoved her right back.

'Hey, cool it, you guys!' someone shouted.

'Bug out, bean-brain!' Judy yelled. She flew at Amanda and shoved her clear across the corridor.

Uh-oh! Amanda had *that* look on her face. She stormed over to Judy and gave her such a shove that she just about *bounced* off the wall.

They looked like they were about to charge each other like a couple of undernourished sumo wrestlers.

So much for Amanda promising Mom that she'd be calm and quiet!

I shoved in between them. Stacy the Brave! Well, I couldn't just stand there while they tore each other into tiny little pieces. What would Mom say if Amanda had to be carried home on a stretcher?

'Now, look, guys,' I began as I tried to keep them apart. 'There's gotta be a reasonable and peaceful way of — erk! Ooof! Glurk! *Gahhhh*!'

I was squished as they flew at one another.

For a few seconds I couldn't tell which way was up as they fought with me sandwiched in between.

Then I heard a man's voice.

'What on earth do you two girls think you're doing?'

Judy and Amanda were unpeeled off me.

'It was *her*!' Amanda howled, struggling against the man's grip. He had a tight hold of her shoulder. 'She started it! Let go of me!'

'Don't believe her!' Judy yelled. 'I didn't do a *thing*!'

'Get your hands off me,' Amanda hollered. 'Who the heck do you think you are, mister?'

'I'll tell you who I am, young lady,' the man said sternly. 'I'm the chairman of the panel of judges here today. And I have to say I'm

139

appalled by this behaviour. I've never seen such a disgraceful display.'

'That's right, Uncle Bob,' Judy crowed. 'You tell her!'

'I'm, talking to both of you, Judy,' said the man.

Uncle Bob? This guy was Judy's *uncle*? Judy's *uncle* was Robert Dorian Phillips, the chairman of the panel of judges! For heaven's sake, no *wonder* she was so sure of winning!

Except that from the look on *Uncle Bob's* face, I didn't get the feeling that Judy was his favourite niece right then.

Mr Phillips glared at Judy and Amanda as he held them apart. And he sure had one ferocious way of glaring. The pair of them went very, very quiet. In fact, the whole place was suddenly totally silent as everyone in the line held their breath to see what would happen next.

'But, Uncle Bob,' Judy whined. 'It really wasn't me.' She pointed at Amanda. 'She just *attacked* me like a crazy person, I didn't do a thing to her, honest!'

'You total liar!' Amanda said.

'That's enough!' Judy's uncle barked in a way that sounded like he wasn't used to being ignored. 'I want you both to come with me.'

He started marching them back down the hallway.

'But it wasn't my fault!' Judy wailed. 'I have to register, Uncle Bob.'

'I don't think *either* of you is the sort of person Mr Appleby would want advertising his products.' Mr Phillips barked. 'I'm going to recommend that you're both disqualified!'

'You can't do that!' I heard Amanda howl as the three of them disappeared back through the blue doors. 'This isn't fair! I demand to speak to your boss! I demand to speak to Mr Appleby! I demand . . .' Her voice faded.

There was a murmur of amazement from the rest of the people in line. The blue doors flapped slowly to and fro and Judy and Amanda's protests got quieter and quieter as they were marched off.

Rachel came up behind me. 'Wow,' she breathed, 'way to blow the contest, Amanda!'

I gave her an expressive look. If it hadn't been for *her* sticking her nose in, the fight between Amanda and Judy might never have started in the first place!

Chapter Fifteen

'OK, everyone,' a voice called from the front of the line. 'The show's over! Let's get registered. Follow me.'

The line began to shuffle along as people went through a doorway. I just *stood* there feeling totally stunned. I almost expected the blue doors to come swinging open and for Amanda to walk through with a big smile on her face and with some explanation of how she'd talked Mr Phillips into letting her back in.

Suddenly the doors did burst open. Amanda? No, *Fern*.

'Whew!' she gasped. 'I only just made it. The car wouldn't start.' She was still dressed up like an explosion in a paint factory. 'Hey,' she said, 'thanks for waiting for me.' She hooked a thumb over her shoulder. 'There was some guy back there with Amanda and Judy. They all looked really mad. Did I miss something?'

'They had a fight,' I said. 'The guy is the

chairman of the judges — and he's Judy's *uncle*! He's disqualified them.'

'Judy's uncle?' Fern said. 'You mean Judy's uncle disqualified *Judy*?' She started laughing. 'That's completely brilliant!'

'He disqualified Amanda, too!' I said. 'I have to go check she's OK.'

'Not *now*,' Fern said. 'A woman out front just told me that everyone has to be registered in the next couple of minutes, Stacy. That's why I was running. The whole thing's just about to start.'

'I can't help that,' I said. 'I have to find Amanda. You know how important this competition is to her. If she's been thrown out she'll be really upset.'

'Yeah,' Fern said in her usual heartless way. 'So?'

'She's my *sister*, Fern,' I said. 'I have to do *something*.'

I ran through the doors and down the stairs to the foyer. There were only a few people left down there, and there was no sign of Amanda, Judy or Mr Phillips.

I asked if anyone had seen them. I was told they'd gone out through the main exit. I ran out front, but I couldn't see them anywhere.

For a few seconds I couldn't think what to do. I knew Amanda would be totally devastated.

143

And then I had a brainwave. James would help! Of course. All I had to do was find James and tell him what had happened. He'd know how to handle it. He'd come up with some way of getting Amanda back in the contest.

I went back in and headed for the red doors. One of the big sports halls had been filled with seats and a stage had been built at one end. Someone on stage was talking through a microphone to the audience as they took their seats, but I was too busy searching for James to hear what they were saying.

I ran up and down the aisles. I saw Pippa and Andy sitting over at the far side, as well as a few other people I knew. But there was no sign of James. Where *was* he?

I ran back into the corridor, getting more and more frantic. Ha! At last! *There* he was! Talking with a large, bald man way down at the far end of the corridor. James was shaking his head but the fat, bald man was nodding and making big gestures with his arms, like some kind of crazy over-enthusiastic windmill.

But while I was still catching my breath, the man put his arm around James's shoulders and the two of them disappeared around a corner.

'James!' I called. 'Wait!'

I ran after them. But just around the corner

there were stairs going up and stairs going down as well as corridors leading off every which way and a whole bunch of doors. James and the fat man could have gone *anywhere*!

'I don't believe this!' I complained to myself.

I heard fanfare-type music from somewhere nearby. I didn't have to be a genius to figure out what *that* meant. The competition had started.

I'd missed out on my chance of being in the finals! For a second I really wished I hadn't chosen to try and find Amanda. But the whole point was that she'd really tried to deal with Judy in a calm, adult way. It had been that prize-winning idiot Rachel who had set the fight off! It hadn't been Amanda's fault.

I walked back into the foyer just as Mom was coming in through the main entrance. She smiled and waved. Then she gave me a puzzled look as she saw that I was so miserable-looking.

'Honey,' she said as I ran over to her. 'What on earth's the matter?'

'Amanda's been thrown out,' I gabbled. 'I can't find James *anywhere*, and I didn't register in time!'

Mom took hold of my shoulders and held me steady.

'OK, sweetheart,' she said calmly. 'Slow down a little and tell me *exactly* what happened.'

★   ★   ★

Five minutes later we were in our car and driving slowly along the route home, on the lookout for Amanda.

'Amanda was handling it really well,' I said to my mom. 'And then that bimbo, Rachel, had to stick her big nose in!'

'Don't call people names, please, honey,' Mom said. 'I don't like it.'

'Rachel is still an idiot whether I *say* so or not,' I mumbled under my breath.

'I just hope Amanda had the sense to walk away from Judy,' Mom said. 'I hope she didn't get into a worse fight.' She sighed. 'Your *sister*!'

'It wasn't her fault at all,' I said. 'And anyway, Judy's such a—'

'Stacy!' Mom said warningly.

'Well, she *is*,' I said. 'She thought she had the whole competition in the bag because of her uncle.'

'She was wrong there,' Mom said. 'Still, at least *something* positive has come out of all of this.'

'It has? Like what?'

Mom smiled. 'You lost out on being in the

finals because you wanted to make sure Amanda was OK,' Mom said. She glanced at me. 'That shows how much you care about her. I'm really proud of you, Stacy.'

'I guess that's true,' I sighed. 'Fern thought I was totally stupid to blow my chances like that.'

'Fern doesn't have a sister,' Mom said. 'She probably doesn't understand how you and Amanda feel about each other deep down.'

'Let's not get too *mushy* here, Mom,' I said. 'I only did it because I didn't have time to think it through properly.'

Mom laughed. 'Don't spoil the moment, Stacy,' she said.

Whatever *that* meant.

'Uh, Mom,' I said after a little while. 'I think maybe I didn't really *mind* missing out on the finals.'

'No?'

I shook my head. 'I don't mean I wouldn't have gone through with it,' I said. 'But it wasn't really my kind of thing, you know? Maybe I went after Amanda so I wouldn't have to take part after all. Maybe it was a good excuse to get out of it.'

'Maybe so,' Mom said. 'Or maybe not. A person can't always tell exactly why they do the things they do. And I'm still really pleased that you— *hey*! There she is!'

Amanda was walking slowly along the pavement with her shoulders slumped and her head down.

Mom tooted the horn and pulled over.

I wound down the window.

'Need a taxi?' I called.

Amanda looked around. Her face was streaked and smeared with tears.

'Hop in, honey,' Mom said. 'We'll take you home.'

Amanda opened the car door and slumped silently into the back seat.

I leaned over the back of my seat.

'You look awful,' I said.

'Thanks a bunch.'

'I tried to find you,' I said.

'Yeah?'

'Amanda,' Mom said over her shoulder as she moved back into the traffic. 'Stacy missed the competition in order to look for you.'

Amanda wiped her hand across her eyes and looked at me. 'You did?' she said.

I shrugged. 'I guess,' I said. 'You don't have to thank me. Just remember it next time you get mad at me. Anyway, what happened with Judy? Did you manage to explain things to her uncle?'

'No,' Amanda sighed. 'He wouldn't listen to a word I said! But I think he was more mad at Judy than he was at me. He kept telling her how disappointed he was in her. Then he took her off somewhere. He said he'd call my parents to come and pick me up, but I said I could get home on my own. The next time I see Judy, I'm gonna take hold of her by the throat and I'm gonna—'

'Yes, OK, Amanda,' Mom interrupted. 'I think we get the picture.'

'Look on the bright side,' I said. 'At least you don't have to quit the cheerleaders.'

'What was that?' Mom said. 'What has the cheerleading squad got to do with anything?'

'I had a little bet with Judy, that's all,' Amanda said. 'It doesn't matter now.'

'Hmmmm,' Mom said. Mom's *hmmms* can be very expressive.

Amanda kept quiet the rest of the way home.

Chapter Sixteen

'I am totally fed up!' Amanda said, slumping onto the couch in our living room. 'Talk about a let-down! This has got to be the most utterly, totally and completely mind-blowingly miserable day of my entire life.' She picked up the remote control and zapped the TV on.

'I missed out, too, don't forget,' I said, sitting next to her.

'Yeah, but you didn't have any chance of winning,' Amanda said. 'It's not the same thing at all.'

I frowned at her. 'You know, you could teach a college level course in *selfishness*, Amanda!' I said. 'Sometimes I just don't *believe* you!'

'Don't yell at me,' Amanda moaned. 'I'm *depressed*.'

'There you go,' Mom said, bringing two plates of cherry pie and ice cream for us. 'See if that makes life worth living.'

'It won't,' Amanda moaned, taking her

plate. 'I'm too upset to eat a single mouthful.' She cut off a huge chunk of pie and stuffed it into her mouth.

The rest of the pie and ice cream vanished the same way. Two minutes later Amanda was asking for another slice.

'Boring!' Amanda said, zapping the TV from channel to channel. 'Boring! Dumb! Seen it! Boring! Boring! Seen it!'

We ended up watching the last hour of part five of some ridiculous mini-series.

I looked at my watch. 'I guess the Blowbubble thing will be finished by now,' I said. 'I wonder who won.'

'I don't care,' Amanda said. 'They probably chose some total idiot. I don't know why I made such a big deal about their dumb competition in the first place.' She got up and started marching around the living room, waving her arms in the air.

'What sort of jerk would want to be seen advertising bubble gum?' she exclaimed. 'I'll tell you something, Stacy, when *I* get my big break, it's going to be for some cool new brand of shampoo or for designer jeans or some really exclusive range of make-up. No way am I going to be seen *dead* advertising bubble gum!'

'It sounds like you've been on the *sour* grape diet, Amanda,' I said.

'Huh?'

Right then the doorbell rang like someone was trying to shove the bell clear through the wall. *Ring-ring-ring-rii-i-i-i-i-i-i-i-ing!*

'Who the heck is *that*?' Amanda said. She marched out into the hall. 'OK, OK,' she shouted. 'I'm coming. Make some more *noise*, why don't you!'

I followed her out.

She yanked the door open. 'What kind of a— oh! James! Fern! Pippa! Andy — will you quit leaning on that *bell*, the door's open already!'

'He won!' Fern yelled. 'He didn't even want to be in it and he *won*!'

I peered around from behind Amanda. The porch was full of excited people.

'Andy *won*?' I said.

'No, not *Andy*!' Pippa yelled.

'What's going on here?' Mom said, coming into the hall.

'I came *second*!' Fern yelled. 'I got a special mention for originality!'

'*Who won*?' Amanda shrieked. 'You said *he* won. *Who* he?'

'*Him* he,' Pippa said, pointing at James.

152

'What?' Amanda's eyes stuck out like golf balls. '*What?*'

'I think you'd all better come in while we hear *this*,' Mom said. 'I didn't even know James had entered.'

'I hadn't,' James said as we herded into the living room. 'I was just about to take a seat when this big guy came up to me and said he wanted to speak to me.'

'It was Thelonius P Appleby!' Andy interrupted. 'Thelonius P Appleby *himself*!'

'The big bald guy?' I said to James. 'I *saw* you with him.'

'Yeah, well,' James said, 'he started telling me about how he'd noticed me because I reminded him of the way *he* looked when he was a teenager.'

'That must have been a few hundred *meals* ago,' Fern said.

'He said I had the *exact* look he wanted,' James said, sounding a little dazed by it all. 'I told him I wasn't even in the competition, but he said he'd fix it for me.'

'You mean he rigged the whole thing so you won?' I said.

'No,' James said. 'He just arranged for me to be in the finals.'

'I thought you weren't interested,' Amanda

gasped. 'I thought you said you'd be too embarrassed.'

'He's very persuasive,' James said. 'He wouldn't take no for an answer. In the end I just went along with it.'

'And he *won*!' Pippa shrieked. 'He's going to be the face on all the Blowbubble commercials for the next twelve months! Isn't that totally brilliant?'

James looked sympathetically at Amanda. 'I'm really sorry about what happened to you,' he said. 'I'm sure you'd have won if you'd been allowed to take part.'

'Forget *that*!' Amanda whooped. 'You *won*! Wow! Wow-wow-wow!' She flung her arms around James and spun him round and round. 'Have I got good taste in boyfriends, or *what*!' she yelled. 'James! You're gonna be *famous*!'

'Wait a minute, Amanda,' I said, laughing at the expression on James's face. 'Not two minutes ago you were telling me that they'd choose an *idiot*, and that only a jerk would want to be seen advertising bubble gum.'

'Oh, Stacy!' Amanda declared breathlessly. 'I said no such *thing*! You just never *listen*! I said that now I was out of it, there were only idiots and jerks in the running—'

'Hey!' Fern yelled. 'Do you mind!'

'I didn't mean you,' Amanda said. 'I meant

all the *other* idiots and jerks. *Anyway*, I was going to say that it was a real shame that James hadn't gone in for it, because with opposition like that, he'd have *walked* it!' She let out another deafening whoop. 'And he *did*! Which proves that not only is he the smartest and best-looking guy in the entire town, but that he's a total star!' She grinned. 'And I've known that all along! I mean, why else would he be going out with *me*?'

I just laughed. Trust Amanda to twist it around so it still sounded like she came out on top.

But then I guess that's the kind of thing you have to get used to when you have a big sister like Amanda!

Other great reads **from Red Fox**

Little Sister Series by Allan Frewin Jones

LITTLE SISTER 1 – THE GREAT SISTER WAR

Meet Stacy Allen, a ten year old tomboy and a bit of a
bookworm. Now meet her blue-eyed blonde sister,
Amanda, just turned 13 and a fully-fledged teenager.
Stacy thinks Amanda's a total airhead and Amanda calls
Stacy and her gang the nerds; they have the biggest love-
hate relationship of the century and that can only mean
one thing – war.
ISBN 0 09 938381 0   £2.99

LITTLE SISTER 2 – MY SISTER, MY SLAVE

When Amanda starts to become a school slacker, Mom
is ready to take drastic action – pull Amanda out of the
cheerleading squad! So the sisters make a deal; Stacy will
help Amanda with her school work in return for two
whole days of slavery. But Amanda doesn't realize that
when her little sister's boss, two days means 48 *whole*
hours of chores – snea-kee!
ISBN 0 09 938391 8   £2.99

LITTLE SISTER 3 – STACY THE MATCHMAKER

Amanda is mad that the school Barbie doll, Judy
McWilliams, has got herself a boyfriend, and to make
things worse it's hunky Greg Masterson, the guy
Amanda has fancied for ages. Stacy feels that it's her
duty as sister to fix Amanda's lovelife and decides to play
cupid and do a bit of matchmaking, with disastrous
results!
ISBN 0 09 938401 9   £2.99

Other great reads ✦ *from Red Fox*

Little Sister Series by Allan Frewin Jones

LITTLE SISTER 4 – COPYCAT

Cousin Laine is so coo-ol! She's a glamorous 18 year old and wears gorgeous clothes, and has got a boyfriend with a car. When Stacy and Amanda's parents go away for a week leaving Laine in charge, 13 year old Amanda decides she wants to be just like her cousin and begins to copy Laine's every move . . .
ISBN 0 09 938411 6   £2.99

LITTLE SISTER 5 – SNEAKING OUT

Pop star Eddie Eden is *the* guy every cool teenager is swooning over and Amanda has got a mega crush on him. Amanda is in love big time and when Eddie's tour dates are announced she's desperate to see her idol – but Mom and Dad don't want her out so late. So what else is there for a love-struck girl to do but sneak out?
ISBN 0 09 938421 3   £2.99

LITTLE SISTER 6 – SISTER SWITCH

Stacy's pen pal, Craig, loves her letters and all his friends are jealous when they see her photo – so he fixes a date. This is bad news for the Allen sisters. Stacy hates her mousy hair and freckles so much that she sent him a photo of pretty Amanda. But if Stacy can persuade Amanda to swop places and be *her* for one day she might be able to keep her secret identity safe . . .
ISBN 0 09 938431 0   £2.99

Other great reads from **Red Fox**

Little Sister Series by Allan Frewin Jones

LITTLE SISTER 7 – FULL HOUSE

When Aunt Susie comes to stay Stacy and Amanda are
forced to – horror of horrors – *share a room*! Naturally
a territorial riot breaks out. Will they be too busy
arguing with each other to notice that Mom and sister
Susie are indulging in a bit of sisterly fireworks of their
own?
ISBN 0 09 966121 7   £2.99

LITTLE SISTER 8 – BAD BOY

No more teen crushes, Amanda is 100% certain, it's true
love with a capital 'L'. *She's* crazy over a gorgeous guy
and *he's* mad about his babe, Amanda. Or is he? When
Stacy spots Amanda's hunk with arch enemy, Judy
MacWilliams, she decides it's time to take some sisterly
action to protect Amanda from a broken heart . . .
ISBN 0 09 966641 3   £2.99

LITTLE SISTER 9 – THE NEW STACY

Something weird is happening to Stacy's girlie gang.
Cindy's taken off to sunny California, Pippa's hanging
out with a *guy* and Fern has disappeared from the social
scene – she's become a work-a-holic! Is befriending
Amanda's Bimbo pals the answer? Lonely heart Stacy
decides the time has come to find out!
ISBN 0 09 966651 0   £2.99

Other great reads *from* **Red Fox**

Little Sister Series by Allan Frewin Jones

LITTLE SISTER 10 – SUMMER CAMP

Summer camp means no school, no homework and . . .
NO AMANDA – bliss! Stacy can't wait to head off for
two whole weeks away from Amanda and the Bimbo
brigade. Then disaster strikes and the Allen sisters end
up at the *same camp*. Now Stacy's suffering in babeland
– and she's cramping Amanda's style big time . . .
ISBN 0 09 968871 9   £2.99

Look out for LITTLE SISTER – STAR SEARCH
coming soon from Red Fox!

LITTLE SISTER 11 – STAR SEARCH

Four Corners's home-grown hero, bubble gum magnate
Thelonius Appleby III, is searching for a girl to star in his
ad campaign. With coast-to-coast fame and super-
stardom in the offing, everyone wants to be *the*
Blowbubble Bubble Gum Girl – but will Stacy and
Amanda be too busy arguing to get chosen? . . .
ISBN 0 09 968881 6   £2.99